JUST AS I AM

Unfailing Love BOOK ONE

MANDI BLAKE

Just as I am
Unfailing Love Book 1
By Mandi Blake

Published in the United States of America.

Cover designer: Amanda Walker PA &
Design Services
Editor: Editing Done Write
Proofreader: Lyssa Dawn

ISBN: 978-1-7337642-0-9

ACKNOWLEDGMENTS

As much as I always wanted to write a book, I never imagined I would actually do it. I owe a great thanks to so many people who have supported me through this big event.

I have the best friends and family who have stood beside me and believed in me. Thank you to Angela Watson for loving books with me, and then loving *my* book with me. I'm not sure I would have ever taken this leap without you. I would have been lost without Ginny Roberts and Tanya Smith. Your encouragement has meant so much to me. I need to give a big thanks to Dana Burttram for answering some of my questions about law enforcement protocol.

I have to thank my husband for encouraging me to take this big step. And it's always a confidence boost when my toddler looks at me in amazement when I tell her I wrote a book.

My lovely editor, Brandi Aquino, has guided me through more than editing. I can't tell you how grateful I have been for her kindness and guidance. I may be biased, but I think Amanda Walker did an *amazing* job on the cover.

Last, but certainly not least, I'm thankful I get to share my love of words and the stories they create with so many lovely readers! I couldn't do this without a community of people who enjoy reading as much as I do.

Note From the Author

I feel the need to make sure you know exactly what you're getting into when you dive into this book.

This book has strong Christian themes and revolves around two main characters who are intent on growing their relationships with God. Sometimes, even Christians find themselves in terrible places in life. This story begins with our main character attempting to escape one of these dangerous situations.

I wanted this story to be a message of hope, a plea to never give up. I also wanted to write a story where the characters weren't pulled apart. I wanted them to choose each other and face the obstacles of life together. There is strength in numbers, and sometimes, God places helpers in our lives to pick us up when we're faltering. With that in mind, I wanted to write a romance full of love but also full of God. It's important to remember that God will always be the first to weather any storm beside us.

I hope you enjoy this story of Declan and Adeline—flawed, yet full of faith and learning every day.

ONTENTS:

PROLOGUE

Adeline dropped another piece of clothing and cursed herself for the delay. She was racing toward a panic attack, and her hands were trembling as she stuffed another shirt into her bag. She would never make it out of here at this rate. Her chest constricted at the thought of what could—no, what *would*—happen to her if she couldn't get her things together and get out of here before Jason got home.

Her heart was still hammering trying to process the new information that had her world turning inside out. She felt stupid for not putting it all together sooner. Shame crowded her when she thought about how blind she'd been all these years. How had she lived with Jason for so long and never really known him? In the beginning, she'd been naive and had trusted him with more than he deserved. She had grown complacent in the years since then, overlooking small pieces of information that had been bright-red flags.

She wondered now if things would have been different had she learned his secret in bits and pieces over time instead of all at once. Would she have formed a better plan to leave him? Would she have confronted him? She couldn't help but think that the escape she was making now would be easier had she been given time to prepare.

She closed her eyes tightly for a moment and wondered how her life had turned out so wrong. She hadn't wanted any of this. Not the relationship, not the lies, not the control he asserted over her life. For years she had been afraid to even think about leaving. She had no money, no job, and no home. How could she possibly make it on her own?

Jason, her boyfriend for six years, the man who controlled every aspect of her life, was not the head of the marketing department at a prestigious firm in downtown New Orleans. No, when he dressed up every morning and worked odd hours of the day and night, he wasn't attending meetings and pushing projects. He was dealing drugs.

Jason had drilled many of his rules into her head from the day they moved in together, but one rule sat above all others: don't ever open the door for anyone.

Until today, following the rule hadn't been an issue. Until today, no one had shown up at their door.

She had been cleaning the dishes after her breakfast for one since Jason hadn't come home last night when a determined fist had begun banging on the door and a man's voice had pierced the apartment, frantic and high pitched.

"Let me in, Jason. I know this is your place. Mike told me. I need some of that stuff from last week quick. I'm dying." The man spoke fast, running his sentences together.

She stopped with the dirty dinner plate hanging in the air above the sink. What should she do? She knew Jason told her not to answer the door, but that man said he was dying.

"Please, Jason, just open the door. I have the money," the man on the other side of the door pleaded, and she waited a heartbeat before his knocking resumed more vigorously, making her jump. "Jason, I mean it. Open this door."

Caution overrode the concern she had felt for the man only a moment ago as he slapped his open hand against the wooden door.

"Come on, Jason. I know you told me not to look for you outside the meeting place, but this is an emergency. I need a fix *now*."

Eventually, the man left after carrying on a conversation with himself and kicking the door. She stood paralyzed, staring at the dirty dishes in the sink for almost five minutes after he left, letting the man's words fill in the blanks she conveniently left gaping in her mind.

She and Jason had never spoken a word to each other about drugs, and the thought had never crossed her mind. She liked to consider herself a smart woman, but that thought had been blown out of the water in light of the revelation. Not to mention a smart woman would have figured out how to get away from Jason by now. He could have implicated her in his crimes, and it seemed he had done so without a bit of remorse.

She scrambled to the tiny bathroom off the living area, quickly getting to her knees and opening the cabinet under the sink. She said a silent prayer that her lifeline was still hidden and expelled a heavy breath when she saw it. She grabbed the tampon box and hugged it to her middle as she tore the top away. The money was still there. A wad of single dollar bills that wouldn't get her far. She hadn't been hiding the money for long enough, and even now it frightened her to think what Jason would do if he knew. A single, silent tear graced her cheek.

A shaky half-laugh escaped her. This box contained the spoils of the years she spent putting back every lone dollar she could get her hands on. She felt confident that Jason would never think of touching a tampon box, but she could never be certain. He was thorough, if nothing else.

She stood and threw the remaining things she owned into the bag hanging from her arm. She swung herself around, made for the bedroom, and grabbed the bag containing the clothes she had already packed.

She didn't have much in this world that was truly hers. The apartment was Jason's. The furniture was Jason's. The car was Jason's. Everything she thought of as hers was really his.

Adeline didn't stop to say goodbye to the place where she had slept every night for the past four years. She hightailed it directly for the door. She never thought of the apartment as home anyway, since Jason wouldn't allow her to put her own touch on the place. Not to mention the awful smell she couldn't seem to eradicate. It seemed to seep from the floors and walls, but she was never allowed to get to know her neighbors, so she had no idea what caused this entire building to smell like rot. She could guess it was mold, but she couldn't be certain.

Her doubts were stacking one on top of the other in her mind, and her fear was growing by the second. She closed her eyes and said a prayer for deliverance as she hitched the bag higher on her shoulder and started for the door. *God, please lead me to safety.* It had been so long since she talked to God, she was afraid to ask for anything. Should she expect Him to carry her through the hard times when she hadn't been the child He wanted her to be lately?

She was about three feet from the door when the sound of Jason's rhythmic footfalls on the stairs momentarily paralyzed her. The echoing blows of his steps were deafening against the silence of the apartment.

Jason was here, and she was too late.

As the panic released her, she lunged for the door, locking the deadbolt and the latch at the top in one fell swoop. She pushed off the door behind her and propelled herself toward the fire escape. She was out the window and down the escape faster than she knew her body could carry her. She couldn't help thinking it was a good thing her flight instinct had chosen this moment to shine.

When she hit the ground, a jolt of pain ran up her shins, and she bit her lip not to let out the string of profanities that threatened to escape. She didn't want to draw attention to herself, in case Jason had made it inside the apartment already. He would know something was wrong, as soon as he realized the thick metal latch was secure and she wasn't coming to the door when he knocked. She had precious few minutes, and he was too smart to let her get far. He'd never hit her before, but she had always been careful to stay on his good side. This was her first act of defiance, and it was a big one.

Brushing her dark hair from her face, she cursed her waist-length tresses for hindering her. Jason hadn't let her cut it, and she had come to loathe her chocolate mane in the years it had been growing wildly.

She thought about the fact that she didn't have a car and briefly considered taking Jason's. She had no doubt that he would report it stolen if she tried to use it to escape.

Stopping for only a beat to take a deep breath, Adeline set out at the fastest run she could manage with the bags bouncing on her back. She had to create space between herself and the apartment so she could figure out a plan.

Pulling her cell from her purse, she quickly connected to Uber and requested a pickup for the bus station. If she was going to use the driver service, it was now or never. She would have to disconnect Jason's credit card as soon as possible. She would also have to ditch her cell phone somewhere between here and wherever she ended up. Breaking the chains of the life she was running away from would have to be thorough.

Two minutes until pickup. In any other situation, she would be praising the quick service. In her current state, two minutes could mean success or failure... possibly life or death.

The older model Ford Taurus hit the curb in front of her as the exhaust struck her nose. She was having trouble breathing through this anyway. What would one more factor hurt?

She slunk into the car, threw her bags onto the seat beside her, and immediately shouted, "Please drive. I'm in a hurry." Thank goodness for this skinny, older man who did just as she asked. He floored it, and she turned around to make sure no one was following her. There was no sign of Jason.

Adeline turned to face forward again, expelling a breath she didn't realize she had been holding. Not only were her hands shaking, but her body seemed to be trembling. Even her teeth were chattering. This must be the leftover adrenaline, the fear that had finally overtaken her weak indifference. She stuck her left index fingernail between her teeth to stop the chattering.

In that moment, she promised herself no more looking back. She was leaving the only life she had ever known, and what's done was done. There would be no going back now.

She wouldn't miss it, for the most part. She had grown to resent Jason and the way he controlled her and every aspect of her life.

Once upon a time, she had been happy—a free, young, spirited girl with only dreams to look forward to in the future. Now, sitting here in this car, driving away from New Orleans, the city she had grown up in, she wondered how her life had gone so wrong.

She loved living in New Orleans and had never imagined she would ever leave knowing this city owned her heart. The parts she would miss had been a foggy memory for a long time now. She had to let it go, but she wouldn't forget this place that she had called home.

A single tear glided down her cheek, and she closed her eyes as the wetness shocked her into the here and now. *Get a grip on yourself! You can do this without falling to pieces. If you let the darkness in, it will tear you apart.*

She pulled herself up to the back of the driver's seat. "Thanks for not asking questions. I know I'm a mess." She took a deep breath and let it out in a rush.

He half turned to look at her. "You look like you're in a hurry to get outta here."

"You could say that." She'd feel a lot more relaxed if she could put some distance between herself and that apartment.

The man's gaze found hers in the rearview mirror. "I'm Paul. It's good to meet you."

Adeline gave a soft smile. She had rarely been allowed to venture outside the apartment, and meeting a friendly face in the middle of the storm she was running from felt like a sign. "I'm Adeline." As an afterthought she added, "You can call me Addie." She didn't know what had prompted her to add the last bit. No one had called her Addie since her mom and dad.

Paul took a left turn on two wheels, and she grabbed onto the seat in front of her. She appreciated his sense of urgency. When the vehicle had righted onto a straightaway, he cocked his head toward her but kept his eyes on the road. "I don't got nothin' else goin' on tonight.

I can be off the clock and take you farther than the bus station."

He sounded so fatherly. She could almost hear her own dad's voice. "You'd do that for me?" Hot tears pricked the back of her eyes at his offer.

Paul looked back at her as he did a rolling stop through an intersection. His voice rang with the uninhibited yat accent of her city. "You look scared, an' if my daughter needed help, I'd hope some nice person would offer. Plus, I'm an old man. I don't do this for the money. Where ya headed?"

She sat back and gave in to another deep breath to ease the tension. With the release of the tightness in her shoulders came a little clarity as she thought for the first time about where she should be going.

"How far east can you take me?" she asked.

"I wouldn't mind a drive to Mobile tonight."

God bless this sweet man. He was willing to drive over two hours through two states. The closer she could get to her final destination in Carson the better. The idea of getting closer to that little town in Georgia gave her a glimmer of hope that she could really do this.

"That sounds perfect. I can't thank you enough." She gave his shoulder a light squeeze.

He nodded, and she picked up her phone. Turning it over in her hands, she realized she hadn't seen her Aunt Karen and Uncle Butch in at least four years, but they were good people and would take her in without thinking twice. They were the salt of the Earth, and her throat constricted with the thought of their unending kindness to her in her younger years.

She hit call, and a smile stole over her face when she heard Aunt Karen's sing-song voice answer, "Hello."

"Hey, Aunt Karen, it's Adeline. I know it's late, but can I come visit for a while?"

CHAPTER ONE

Two Months Later
Declan

Declan King strode deliberately toward the back offices of the hardware store. His first stop this morning was a visit with his friend, Brian, the sales manager and co-owner of the hardware store. It was good to know people in the right places.

His friend and business partner, Dakota, was handling a meeting with a homeowner and a subcontractor this morning. He was more than happy to let Dakota handle the meetings in their business. A clash between the working parties had been keeping everyone from meeting deadlines for almost a week now, but he was going to assume he would get the go-ahead for the flooring they had already discussed.

Declan had taken a roundabout tour through the store, making sure to use the areas with the least amount of foot traffic. The last thing he wanted to do this morning was run into someone who wanted to chitchat.

He didn't like talking to people at all, if he could help it. He just... didn't interact well with most people. He wasn't really the happy-go-lucky kinda guy. Never had been, but his instinct to steer clear of the chatter had grown worse lately.

But, of course, he wouldn't be so lucky. He turned the corner in the grilling section to find Butch and Karen Jackson bantering over charcoal versus gas grills. It was too late. His heavy boots were loud against the concrete floor, and they spotted him just as he tried to turn back.

"Declan! Hey there." Karen waved merrily with a smile on her face. "It's so good to see you. We need your help." Karen reached for his hand, pulling him toward their grill candidates.

Declan despised social interaction, but Butch and Karen were about as easy as he could have hoped for. He actually liked the Jacksons. They were good people. He was the one with the problem.

Karen Jackson was middle-aged and motherly, despite the fact that she and Butch never had children of their own. She had taught half the town in elementary school, including him.

"Yeah, Dec. Would you choose a gas grill over old-fashioned charcoal?" Butch asked as he crossed his arms over his chest. It was easy to tell how the teams had formed around here, but he really hated choosing sides, especially between two people he liked. He could make battlefield decisions in a split second, but his opinion was more difficult to share.

"Um, well, charcoal gives a good flavor, but gas is easier," Declan admitted as he brushed his open palm against the scruff on his cheek.

"You're not answering the question, Mr. King." There it was. Karen's teacher voice. He might as well be seven years old again.

He scratched his head and studied the grill choices. "I'd personally go with charcoal. I prefer the flavor, and I don't mind devoting a little extra time to watching and maintaining it while it's cooking."

Karen uncrossed her arms and turned to Butch. "Is that the one you really want?" She was conceding, but he could hear in her tone that she wanted to make sure her husband was getting what he wanted.

"Yes, honey. I promise you'll love it. I'll cook steaks tonight to celebrate." Butch wrapped an arm around his wife's shoulders and pulled her in to plant a kiss on the side of her graying hair.

Karen grinned through her blush and remembered Declan. "So what have you been up to lately, Mr. King? I haven't seen you in years, but I heard you were back in town." He noticed that people in Carson acted like he had been dead for eight years, instead of working for the United States Army. Out of sight, out of mind.

Karen's eyes held a soft kindness. "We're so sorry about your grandparents. They were good people. They lived good, long lives. Not to mention they were so proud of you. Bragged about you all the time." Her southern drawl was accentuated in her remorse. She touched his arm, and he wiped his sweating palms on his jeans. If anyone else had touched him, he would have recoiled on instinct.

What he wouldn't give to be anywhere else right now. Was it getting hotter in here? Talking about himself or his family was worse than giving his two cents on a grill. "I'm doin' fine, Mrs. Jackson. The farm is keepin' me busy, and I plan to get around to going through their house soon." That wasn't really the whole truth, but *soon* was a relative term.

Karen's eyes grew round and he could practically see the lightbulb shining over her head. He couldn't even guess at the plan she had just concocted.

"You know what?" She swatted Butch's arm playfully with the back of her hand. "I bet Addie would like to help him go through all that stuff."

Hold the phone. Who was Addie? He was sure he hadn't asked for help. He was a one man show and always preferred to work alone.

Before he could protest, Butch replied, "Oh, I know she would." He turned to Declan and gave him a good once-over, like he was judging a prize pig at the county fair. "Have you met our Addie?"

Declan stuck his hands securely in his pockets. How much longer did he have to keep talking? "I can't say I have."

Karen leaned into her husband's side as she picked up the explanation. "You see, Addie is our niece. She just moved in with us from Louisiana. She's had a bit of a rough go lately, and she's having some trouble making friends and stuff."

Butch stepped up to the plate next. "What Karen is trying to say is Addie has an ex-boyfriend who may or may not be trouble." Karen swatted at Butch again and wrinkled her brow.

Butch's tone was soft as he explained, "Honey, there's no sense in beatin' around the bush. You and I both know Declan won't gossip about it."

Declan switched his weight to the other leg and looked behind him to see if maybe there was a way out of this conversation. "Right, I won't tell anyone." And he truly had no intention of sharing their secret. He hadn't even known they had a niece staying with them, so he could understand their secrecy. What he didn't understand was what they wanted from him besides grill advice.

Karen turned on the charm as she explained, "It's just that she's been worried he'll come after her. The poor girl can't stop lookin' over her shoulder. Would you mind ridin' by her work and peekin' in on her every once in a while? It would mean a lot to me." He could see how Karen could get her way in most situations. It was hard to tell her no.

"Where does she work?"

"She's the new receptionist at the salon downtown." He noticed that Karen pointed north, while downtown Carson was definitely southeast.

"How long did you say she's been here?" Declan asked.

Butch leaned against the shelf housing grill accessories. "About two months now."

Really, they weren't asking a lot. He needed a haircut anyway. He could stop by, check out the salon, make sure some crazy ex-boyfriend wasn't bothering her, and be on his way.

"Sure, I can stop by."

Butch's hand came down hard on Declan's shoulder. "Thanks, son. We really appreciate it. Call us if you ever need anything. Oh, and ask Addie to help you with your grandparents' house. She'll be glad to help."

"I will."

He hugged Karen and shook hands with Butch, but the older man kept his tight grip longer than usual to gain his full attention. "Take care of her, son." Just as fast as it had appeared, the seriousness was gone as Butch winked and turned to join his wife.

Declan resumed his trek to Brian's office and wondered why the Jacksons had practically pushed their niece on him. If she was having trouble making friends, maybe she would understand he wasn't the best person to help anyone integrate in a new place.

He knew he wasn't the right person to help their niece, but he'd made a promise, and now he was committed. This wasn't the first time he'd found himself stuck in a situation he shouldn't be in because he hadn't known how to say the right thing at the right time.

Rubbing a hand over his face, he resigned himself to the inevitable and hoped the Jacksons would forgive him when he let them down.

CHAPTER TWO

Declan

He finished up the day's work around six-thirty that evening and remembered his promise to check in on the Jacksons' niece. There were plenty of daylight hours left, but he was dripping sweat. The August heat was unrelenting, and he was filthy.

After running home for a shower and change of clothes, he headed back into town for the haircut he had been putting off. He parked his work truck against the sidewalk on downtown Carson's Main Street. The only salon in town was hard to miss.

Declan tapped the heel of his boot on the floorboard of his 1986 Chevy Silverado. The truck had been his grandfather's, and he had formed an attachment to it since coming home.

He tried to motivate himself to get out of the truck. He hated going out in public for anything. A haircut, groceries, the bank, it didn't matter. Typically, the hardware store was tolerable, but he wouldn't even be caught there without a reason.

He took a deep breath, adjusted his Georgia Bulldogs baseball cap, and stepped out into the street. The law offices that blanketed the streets surrounding the courthouse square had closed up shop, but the small "entertainment district" made up of a brewery, a Mexican restaurant, and a dive bar a few blocks down was just winding up.

It was 7:30 before he heard the bell chime above his head as he entered the salon. Chairs lined the window wall that faced Main Street, and shelves holding tubes and bottles in every color filled the opposite wall. An enormous circular mirror framed in an ornate dark wood covered a smaller wall, and an unobtrusive receptionist desk sat on the remaining side of the room to his left.

This was a far cry from the barber shop on the north side of town he always used. He had just stepped into the women's version of the haircut experience. Neil ran a decent barber shop, but he could understand why his establishment didn't appeal to women after seeing the competition. Although, he had to give props to Neil's place. The musk and spice of the barber shop sure smelled better than the chemicals that filled his nose now.

The room was empty, but the ding of the bell had prompted shuffling in the back room. He shifted his weight back and forth and stuck his hands in his pockets to wait.

He barely had time to give the room another scan before a tall brunette rounded the corner with a smile that overtook her entire face. "Hey, sorry about that. I just stepped into the back to grab some shampoo to restock."

She was gorgeous. From her brilliant blue eyes to her easy smile, she was a walking, talking beauty. The woman wore a black scoop neck top that cinched at her waist and flowed out around her hips and white pants. Her clothes projected a more reserved personality, but even neutral colors and modest clothing couldn't hide her innate beauty.

Carson was a small town, and Declan may not have been the best at holding conversation, but he was an exceptional listener. He had made it his business to know what went on here since he moved back. He didn't repeat the things he heard, but he definitely knew most of the comings and goings.

This woman was something he shouldn't have missed.

He tilted his chin to the floor and adjusted his cap. Good grief, he had been able to tackle dangerous situations at a moment's notice less than a year ago in the Army, but he couldn't open his mouth and speak to a beautiful woman.

"What can I help you with today?" Even her voice was like a song. He'd bet his last paycheck she could sing.

All at once, his internal struggle became clear. Some part of him hoped she was Butch and Karen's niece, while the other part of him knew their request to look in on their niece would prove more difficult if he couldn't pull himself together in front of her. Scratching the side of his neck, he asked, "Are you Addie?"

Her smile faltered a bit, but she didn't let it slip completely. "Yes. Do I know you?"

When her mood changed, he remembered Butch and Karen telling him their niece had been worried that an ex-boyfriend was looking for her. Now here comes a stranger asking questions.

For the first time today he wondered if he was supposed to mention the errand Butch and Karen had sent him on. How would she feel about her aunt and uncle asking someone to watch out for her?

"I'm Declan King, a friend of Butch and Karen. I ran into them at the hardware store today, and they suggested I stop by for a haircut. You know Karen, she's always looking out for people." He removed his cap and ran a hand through his noticeably shaggy hair. "Seems like I'm a little overdue for a trim."

He gave her the best smile he could manage, and her own smile returned. "Well, we can definitely take care of that for you. It's nice to meet you, Declan. I'm Adeline Rhodes, but you can call me Addie."

Rhodes. She must be Butch's sister's daughter. He didn't know many Rhodes that lived in Carson, and it was easy to know everyone in this small town.

"Nice to meet you too." He was starting to see why Butch had sized him up. If Addie was single, he could smell a matchmaking. He had known Karen most of his life, and she should know by now that he wasn't good boyfriend material. Karen had watched him stammer through his third-grade year, and he hadn't changed much since. He was still that same socially awkward person, just eighteen years older.

But a woman as sweet and beautiful as Adeline Rhodes made him pray a man could change his ways.

She stood and gestured for him to follow her. "Right this way, and I'll get you set up with Libby."

Wait. Libby? Surely it wasn't *the* Libby Thomas he had known in school. He followed Addie with a sinking feeling he was about to come face to face with his worst nightmare.

"Libby, Declan here needs a trim." Addie gave a sweeping gesture to a fancy black chair, and Declan took his seat.

His head pounded in time with the squeal as the loudest woman he had ever met made her grand entrance. "Declan King!" How had she stretched his last name for three full seconds? "Is that really you? In the flesh?"

"Yep." No way. There was no way this was happening.

Libby wrapped him in a face-on hug and yelled directly in his ear. "It's so good to see you again!"

"So you two know each other." Addie hadn't said it as a question. He could guess that Libby Thomas knew everyone in town on the same friendly basis. He'd spoken a total of ten words to Libby in his life, but her never-ending stream of consciousness had haunted him for years.

There were people who understood his introversion, and there were people who thought they could change him if they were friendly enough. Libby was one of the latter. She'd never given up on him, never given him a moment's peace, and kept him completely uncomfortable all through school.

"Oh, we go way back. We've known each other since we started school, right, Dec?"

He knew the drill. Let her lead and just nod along.

"I can't believe you're back. It's been what, ten years since you left us?"

He knew the window for nodding along was over when she approached his head with the scissors. "Eight."

Libby giggled and playfully swatted his shoulder. "I can't believe you didn't even visit."

"Where have you been?" Addie asked as she sat in a chair across the room. She was still just inside his field of vision, and he thanked God for little blessings. Something about her sitting there made this event tolerable.

Libby answered for him. "The Army. Dec here is our hometown hero. Just look at these muscles." She showed no shame as she flung the cape aside and gripped his upper arm with her plump fingers tipped with manicured fire engine red nails. He closed his eyes and silently recited the *Pledge of Allegiance* to distract himself while Libby resumed his trim. What he wouldn't give to be at home right now.

Addie's sweet voice had him opening his eyes. "Really? So you traveled a lot?"

He took a deep breath. "Yeah, I guess you could say that." *Please don't ask. Please don't ask.* He really couldn't talk about the Army right now.

"I've only been to New Orleans and here," Addie confided.

Before he knew it, Declan found himself asking, "Why New Orleans?"

Addie sat up straighter and smiled. "It's where I'm from. I just moved here a few months ago."

Right, the Jacksons had mentioned she was from out of town. From the proud look he saw in her eyes, he could tell she had loved her old home. A part of him hated that she had been forced to leave, but another selfish part of him was glad she was here with him.

"When did you decide to go full-on mountain man, Dec? This beard needs some serious attention." Libby tugged at his beard, and he couldn't help the recoil at her touch. Had she really just touched his face? Libby had no boundaries.

"It's new." What kind of conversation did she expect him to carry on about his beard?

She turned to her shelf of products and grabbed one that seemed random. "Well I'm going to have to trim it up and make it look nice if you're plannin' on keepin' it. This is not gonna fly around here. I can't let you go around tellin' people I cut your hair and have them see that I let you walk outta here with this mess." She waved a hand in front of his face to indicate his beard.

"Um… I promise I'll shape it up when I get home." He wasn't above jumping over the back of this chair if she didn't let it go.

"Fine, suit yourself. I'm just tryin' to make you look better." She batted her eyelashes and smiled as she said, "Not that you need any help, doll." She pursed her lips to the side and winked at him.

He snuck a glance at Addie to find her hand covering her mouth and her shoulders shaking as she tried to control her giggles. Her eyes lit up, and he wondered why her presence didn't seem to bother him as much as usual.

Libby flicked the black cape from his shoulders and brushed the loose hairs from his neck. "You're free to go. Addie will take care of you up front."

"Thanks, Libby."

Libby twisted her head back and forth, showcasing her features in profile. Her dark-red hair swayed around her face. He noticed she wore a lot of makeup. Libby had always been pretty, but she erred toward the dramatic side. "Don't be a stranger. I expect to see you in here within the next decade. Understood?"

"Sure. See you soon."

Addie popped up from her seat with extra bounce and a smile as she led him back to the desk at the front of the store.

"Did you enjoy your salon experience today, Mr. King?" He could tell she was onto him, and he liked that she wasn't taking his discomfort too seriously. Declan hated the times when his problem made other people just as uncomfortable as him.

"Define *enjoy*."

She gave a laugh and let him off the hook. "Libby's fun, isn't she?"

He smiled and pulled out his wallet, feeling the stress of being trapped in Libby's chair leave his shoulders. "If you say so."

He paid her for the haircut and remembered the other bit of advice Karen and Butch had shared with him today.

"So, I have a project that I need to work on, and I kinda need some help. Butch and Karen seemed to think I could ask you…" Now that he started the conversation, he didn't really know how to ask her to help clean out his dead grandparents' house.

Addie leaned over the desk, waiting for his proposal, and he caught the scent of vanilla and… something that reminded him of home.

"Okay. What can I do to help?"

His mind was blank. What had he been asking? "Um, well…" He rubbed his neck as he tried to think of the words.

"You see, I didn't reenlist for the Army because my grandparents died this year."

Addie sat up straight and her smile fell. "I'm so sorry to hear that."

"Thanks. Really, I've been doing a minimal job keeping up the farm while I work, and I haven't gotten a chance to go through their house and get it ready to sell." He still wasn't sure he wanted to sell the house. He was living in his old family home on the same property, and he liked that his closest neighbors were a quarter of a mile away.

"Karen and Butch said you might be able to help me. I can pay you."

She shook her head. "You don't need to pay me. I'll help out for free."

A brilliant idea popped into his head. "How about I pay you in meals? Breakfast, lunch, and dinner. Anywhere you want in town or a home-cooked meal."

Wait, why had that idea seemed so appealing? He had never had the urge to share a meal with anyone. He always felt better when he was alone. Yet, he had been talking to the beautiful Adeline Rhodes and hadn't felt the urge to run.

Addie's whole face blushed a light pink and she fiddled with a pen on the desk. "Okay. We can do that." He could tell she was wondering if he had just proposed a date, but he wasn't ready to answer that yet. If things went well, maybe they *would* be dates.

"Great. Can I pick you up tomorrow? It's supposed to rain, and my job comes to a halt when the weather acts up."

"Sure, I'm staying with Butch and Karen. I can give you the address."

"I know where they live."

"Of course." She rolled her eyes. "I forgot everyone in Carson knows them."

She followed him to the door and waved goodbye as she turned the *OPEN* sign on the door to *CLOSED*.

He sat parallel parked on Main Street and manually rolled the window down in his old truck. The hot summer breeze felt nice against the heat of the day. The sun was setting behind him, and he felt more at peace than he had in months. He propped his arm on the open window and watched the townspeople walking the streets, mostly on their way to dinner.

His phone buzzed with a text in his pocket. It was his friend, Brian.

Dakota is calling you. Don't say no.

Great. He knew what was coming, and he didn't like it one bit. Right on cue, the phone rang in his hand.

Declan answered, "Hey, man. How'd it go?" Dakota was one of the few people he could talk to without getting sweaty palms or hives.

"Awful. Glad it's Friday and we don't have to talk about it until Monday. I need to forget that meeting ever happened. Why can't people just get along and make my job easier? I'll admit I don't like that sub's attitude either, but that homeowner needs to get over her problems with him so we can just build the house already."

"Please tell me at least something got approved." He wasn't a fan of sitting around waiting for the go-ahead when he could be finishing up the project.

"Not a thing. I'm 'bout tired of this petty bickering."

"Amen, brother."

"It's poker night. You're coming." Dakota wasn't one to take no for an answer. He just assumed the answer was yes.

Declan had known Dakota since they were in elementary school together. They were inseparable until Declan left for basic. Eight years later, his friend acted like he had never left.

After spending the majority of the last decade in combat mode or in the wilderness searching for terrorists, friendship wasn't something that came easy anymore. In fact, it was straight-up difficult, and Dakota knew exactly why he was having trouble adjusting. Instead of approaching the elephant in the room head-on, Dakota took a sneak-around-the-bush tactic and avoided the problem.

He knew Dakota was looking for ways to take his mind off the past by picking right up where they left off, hanging out every Friday and Saturday night. Declan just didn't have the hang of it quite yet.

"Sorry, man. I've got some work to do at the house." He glanced toward the salon again and knew Dakota would see through the excuse.

Dakota paused, and his tone was irritated when he finally spoke. "Fine. Maybe next time. It's just, all you do is work. I mean, I work from dawn 'till dark, but at least I use the afterhours to have fun."

Declan rubbed his beard with his free hand, causing a scratching sound. Maybe Libby was right about his facial hair. "I'll come around. I promise I'll work on it. It's just…" He searched for the way to explain to his friend what was really going on. "I don't know how to be a civilian anymore. It's different here."

Dakota let out a short laugh. "No, Ian didn't know how to be a civilian when he came back. He still hasn't gotten his attitude straight."

Declan let out a deep laugh. He knew exactly what Dakota was talking about. Their friend, Ian, was a no-nonsense kind of guy, and the military had only exacerbated that personality trait. Dakota's carefree ways didn't always jibe with Ian. "Yeah, I know what you mean. I'm going to make it my mission to integrate better than Ian."

"That's good enough for me, brother."

As he hung up the call, he tossed the phone into the cup holder and his baseball cap into the passenger seat before running both hands roughly over his face and through his short, brown hair.

He couldn't keep ditching his friends like this. It really wasn't fair to them, since they hadn't done anything except try to help him. It also wasn't fair to them that he wasn't the life of the party anymore, even around his life-long friends. He wouldn't be good company, and that was part of the reason he wasn't eager to rejoin them. They were better off without him. They just didn't know it. He had spent years distancing himself from people and focusing on his job and staying alive.

His past was full of loss, and somehow, he had chosen a career where his co-workers had a higher chance of dying on the job. He had started his job with the U.S. Army after losing his mother and getting close to anyone after her death seemed useless.

He looked toward the salon once more and wondered what kind of a man would be trying to scare or hurt Adeline. She seemed too happy to have a weight like that sitting on her shoulders. The thought of someone hurting her sent a stab like a knife to his gut.

Butch and Karen had asked him to keep an eye out for her, and he took their request to heart now that he had met her. He didn't like the thought of some ex-boyfriend following her around one bit.

Wait. She said she was from New Orleans. Did she think this old boyfriend had followed her here all the way from Louisiana? Was this guy the reason she left New Orleans?

He cracked his knuckles as his imagination ran wild. Maybe he would just stick around until Addie and Libby closed up shop. He didn't have anywhere else to be tonight. He would just sit here and listen to the radio for a few more minutes.

Making sure Addie made it home all right sounded like the best way to make sure he slept easy tonight.

CHAPTER THREE

Adeline

Adeline began cleaning up the salon for closing at 8:00 PM sharp. Looking outside at the ample daylight left, the tension in her shoulders eased a little knowing she should be able to get out of here before nightfall. After two months of hiding, she still couldn't convince herself to let her guard down to the fact that Jason could be looking for her.

She knew better than most people that Jason didn't give up on the things he wanted. She was sure that if he was looking for her, it would be easy for him to assume she would run to her aunt and uncle. She had mentioned them and their home in Carson, Georgia many times over the years they were together.

If he was looking for her, she knew it wasn't because he wanted her back in his life. Oh no, he would be out for her head, and that's why she had taken great pains to stay out of the spotlight.

She told Karen the whole story the night her aunt had picked her up in Mobile, Alabama two months ago. Karen had listened intently as Addie choked through tales of regret and shame spanning the years since the two had really spoken of anything that mattered. Karen was gracious enough to let her finish before patting Addie's hand and saying, "Well, it's water under the bridge now, right, Addie? What matters is that you're safe. Let's get you home now. I'm tired from just hearing your story."

She slept the rest of the ride home. The next day, Karen had taken her to the salon for a professional treatment. They agreed that she would have to change her appearance to some extent in case Jason came looking. She wanted to do anything to make it harder for him to find her. She didn't want to be a shining beacon in the dark for him.

Adeline would remember that day with her aunt for the rest of her life. She didn't know if she had ever been pampered like that before, and the feeling was bliss. When the stylist asked her about the cut she wanted for her hair, she proudly explained exactly what she wanted.

She had dreamed of a makeover for years now, but it hadn't gone further than that. Just dreams. Seeing herself in the mirror hours later with shorter, shining hair brought tears to her eyes. She looked like a completely different person, and she immediately thought this was the person she wanted to be—someone new and of her own choosing. She had a style of her own with a new hope for the future. She hadn't realized she was missing her freedom so much until she saw her dark-brown locks falling to the floor like shackles.

She left the salon with a bright outlook on life, but not before asking for a job application. Becoming financially independent was the first step to making her own path in life, and she was ready to make her mark on this world. Getting the call from the manager later that day with the news that their receptionist was quitting to become a stay-at-home mom and she could start work in the morning was a bonus. She would start off answering the phones, sweeping, making appointments, and washing towels, but the manager encouraged her to consider pursuing a career in cosmetology. They were planning to expand soon and were in need of another stylist. If things worked out, she could have her own station one day.

She was hitting the ground running. She signed up for the classes she needed to begin her cosmetology certification and never looked back. She had started classes two weeks ago, and she was sure this was the path for her. After the memorable makeover that marked the beginning of a new life for her, Adeline knew she wanted to share that life-changing feeling with others.

She couldn't have found a place better than Carson if it had been picked just for her. She was quickly growing to love the people she worked with, and they treated her like family. The change that had come over her life since leaving New Orleans was drastic and wonderful.

The manager of the salon, Helen, was understanding of her school schedule and never gave her grief about the hours she could or couldn't work. Amy was a stylist, and she was always willing to let her watch and learn from her. She couldn't express how much Amy's unofficial lessons had helped her with her schoolwork already.

Then there was Libby, the natural red-haired wild child. She always found ways to have fun or entertain herself, whether it be dancing with the clients—or a broom if no one was available—or "testing" out the new makeup from the makeover counter on herself. Libby was the kind of person who made your soul come alive by being near her. She loved the happiness Libby carried with her and was already starting to look at her co-worker as a true friend.

The people and the job had all just fallen into place after she ran. Everything was coming up roses, but she couldn't shake the small voice in the back of her head that piped up from time to time saying, *This isn't your home. You aren't safe here.*

Months of looking over her shoulder had instilled a natural distrust of strangers, but she couldn't stop thinking about Declan King. What a pleasant surprise he had been this evening. She would have to ask Butch and Karen about him tonight. She told herself she needed to know more about him if she would be helping him with his grandparents' house, but she knew deep down that she was interested in learning more about him for different reasons.

He had a striking presence, but she could tell he shied away from attention. He was tall and broad shouldered with eyes a shade darker and more alluring than her own cornflower blue irises.

She was singing along with the country song on the radio when Libby stopped her on her way to get the broom from the hall closet.

"Girl, I've got a hot date tonight, and I was wondering if you could close up shop so I can get ready. I look a mess, and I *really* want this one to stick, you know?" Libby didn't play games. If the thought popped into her head, it was coming out of her mouth.

"No problem. I can take it from here." Closing up shop wasn't anything new, and she had a key.

"I owe you big time." Libby's smile was huge and contagious. "I'll take over when you have a date. Speaking of, what did you think about Declan King? He's still a looker after all these years. You know, most men let themselves go when they get close to thirty."

She really didn't want to talk about her aversion to dating. At all. Ever. "I'm not really looking to date right now. You know I wouldn't have time with school and work."

It was only half the truth. If she was being honest, Jason had ruined her to the idea of happy relationships. The one thing that had started breaking her resolve was Butch and Karen's relationship. They were still sweet as pie after twenty-five years together.

"Oh no, girl. You need a man. I'm going to find you one. Give me two days." Her voice went from high-pitched to deep and serious at the end.

Adeline quickly sputtered, "No, no, no. Really, I'm fine. Please, I'm... not ready."

She saw the realization in Libby's eyes a moment too late. Libby knew that there was more to the story than she was being told. She had to stop being so jumpy. She wasn't ready to talk about it yet.

After a heavy pause and a side glance, Libby conceded. "All right, I'll let it go for a while, but you let me know when you're ready, and I can make it happen." Libby turned her back on Adeline with a wink and strode to the break room to grab her purse.

It's true that the people you meet are all fighting their own internal battles. She was reminded of her own inadequacy every time someone questioned her about why she was still on the market.

She wasn't oblivious to the fact that most people her age were married with children. She was finding that what constituted "society" in a small southern town looked at her as if she were defective for being single at twenty-four years old. There must be some reason she hadn't been able to snag a man by now. While she was still trying to adjust to her new label of spinster, the whispers and backhanded comments about her lack of romantic entanglement had become annoying.

She called after her friend, "Thanks, Libby. Hope your date goes well."

Libby turned at the door and gave her a wicked smile. "Don't you worry about me, girlfriend. I got this."

She couldn't help the smile that crept onto her face at that farewell. Libby was a character, and it warmed her heart to see someone so carefree and full of life. Maybe one day she would be as confident and energetic as Libby. She could feel the seeds of excitement growing in her. The urge to rejoin the world she had been locked away from grew a little every day.

As the bell dinged on the door at Libby's departure, Adeline fell into a routine as she closed up shop. Her thoughts wandered to her new life path, and she couldn't help chiding herself again for the way she had let Jason control her for so long. She was meant to be free, and she knew that without a doubt now. Jason had suffocated her with his control for too long. She was smarter and stronger now, and she knew a man would never rule her life again. She had seen the light, and there was no going back into the darkness.

It was a miracle she had made it out, really. She had prayed off and on over the years to be free of him, but she hadn't truly thought the day would come. Shaking her head, she chided herself for her lack of faith in God's ability to deliver her from her struggles.

She bagged up the day's garbage and started out the side door of the salon leading to the dumpster in the alley. She knew to make this quick because the sun would be down any minute now, and she wanted to be safely on her way home when darkness fell.

Before her third footfall into the alley, strong arms grabbed her from behind and she dropped the garbage bag. She sucked in a terrified breath as her chest pounded with the realization that her worst fears had caught up to her. She hadn't been careful enough, and she would pay for it in blood.

The nightmare she had been running from all this time was pressing his chest into her back and had a blood-constricting grip across her chest and over her mouth. It was hard to believe there had been a time when Jason had touched her in tenderness. She told herself that years ago he hadn't been so selfish and cruel, but had he truly ever cared for her or shown her kindness? It seemed so far from the truth that held her captive now. She had only ever been a pawn in a world where Jason wanted control.

She attempted to struggle free for a moment and his grip shifted to her shoulders. She screamed as soon as his hand released her mouth, but the call for help was short-lived as he picked her up off her feet and slammed her onto the ground. Her head and shoulder hit the ground hardest, and stars fluttered in the outskirts of her vision. Then her body stopped taking orders from her brain as she silently screamed for her limbs to fight back. She had the will to fight—that self-preservation that screamed to make it stop—but she didn't have the strength to execute it.

Jason rolled her onto her stomach with a jerk and growled behind her ear through his teeth, "What were you thinking running from me?"

Using his body weight to restrain her with one hand on the back of her head, he forced her face into the broken concrete. His fingers splayed through her hair, palming her head like a basketball. She sucked in a mouth full of dirt and coughed harshly through the pain.

This couldn't be happening. No one could be pulled from contentment so quickly. One minute your heart is full of hope and excitement, the next minute you're struggling to survive. She could have sworn there were still faint rays of sunset left in the sky only a few seconds ago. Now the alley was as dark as midnight.

"And what have you done to yourself? I told you not to cut your hair!" He was shouting while she barely had the strength to comprehend the words he was saying as he fisted his hand in her hair and pummeled her head against the ground for emphasis. She hadn't realized just how often God had heard her prayers all those years until the ugly truth hit her in the face.

He jerked his hand from the tangled mess of her hair, and she tried to use her right elbow and left hand to lift herself off the ground. Small pebbles of gravel stuck to her face, and she could taste the blood mixed with dirt on her lip as a shaky voice she didn't recognize came from her constricting throat. "Please stop." It was all she could plead. There was no way she could fight him off. She knew his strength. He was twice her size. His ambush had taken away any slight chance she might have had.

He threw her onto her back and towered over her, bending close to her face. "No way. You won't get pity from me. What were you thinking? After all I've done to support you over the years, this is how you repay me? You couldn't make it without me!" She winced as his spit pelted her face, and her lip quivered. "Did you think I'd just let you leave? Did you think I wouldn't find you?"

Jason's brown hair looked black, bathed in the darkness of the alley as it fell into his eyes. He pulled a knife out of his jacket and covered her mouth with his other hand. Her eyes sprung wide as his intentions became clear. She tried to push her voice past the dirty hand covering her mouth, but it was hopeless. No one would hear her.

When Jason was thrown away from her as swiftly as a rag being tossed aside, she couldn't understand what was happening.

A stranger, shrouded in darkness, grappled with Jason. She fought to keep her focus, but she was fading into a haze. She heard grunts and the meaty sound of flesh connecting with flesh, but she couldn't seem to see what was happening.

It wasn't long before the stranger appeared in front of her and spoke in a rushed, deep voice. "Are you hurt? Can you move?"

She knew that voice. Declan, the man she had met less than an hour ago, was the one who had stopped Jason from hurting her or worse.

She couldn't form a response. She thought it seemed like a simple question, but words wouldn't come. Her head was just... blank.

"You're in shock." He looked over her head at something, and the baseball cap he wore cast a pitch-black shadow over his face.

"We gotta go. Stay with me." He grunted as he hoisted her into his arms in one quick swoop and ran at a jarring pace. She tried to hang on to his shoulders, but she felt the weight of her body sink into him, and her arm slipped from his shoulder down his chest.

Why was her body useless? She let him cradle her, and it felt like he was carrying all of her worries along with her limp body. The acceptance of defeat mingled with the physical blows she had just taken, and she wanted to give up.

She hadn't been held in comforting arms in years, and the sentiment felt foreign. The warmth radiating from Declan's body was filling her up, reminding her that positive touch like this was necessary for happiness. She had been starved without knowing. How had she been deprived of this basic comfort for so long and survived?

She vaguely thought she should be more cautious about a stranger swooping in to save her like he did, but she couldn't find it in her heart to care right now.

She was fading fast, and she knew she didn't have the strength to fight much longer. She found a moment of release in the last seconds of consciousness, but a vague tingling in the back of her mind whispered, *You're safe now. Trust me.*

CHAPTER FOUR

Declan

Declan ignored the searing pain in the right side of his abdomen as he pushed himself to run faster. After knocking the man unconscious, he had crouched down to check on Adeline just as another man rounded the far corner of the alley. It only took him a second to assess the wound in his abdomen and know that he couldn't protect Adeline and himself from this man after being stabbed.

He grabbed her into his arms and ran for his truck. He had made a quick call to Cherokee County deputy Jake Sims, as soon as he heard the scream coming from the alley beside the salon. He had given his friend Jake a hasty summary of what he knew and prayed his friend could make it in time to help.

Right now, Adeline's condition was his top priority. He left the man to be found by either the sheriff's department or the approaching man and ran with her.

Declan had been watching her, and he had still let her ex get too close to her. He thought he would be able to protect her by keeping such a close eye on her, but he had grossly underestimated this man. He had been too busy watching her to notice that the man she had been worried about had already found her and had been waiting for the right moment to strike. The attack had come as a shock, but Declan's instincts had kicked into gear quickly.

Now she was in his arms, and he could feel how vulnerable she was. Her skin was smooth, and she certainly wasn't made of scars and hard muscle like him.

Declan knew the man was following them, so he practically threw her into the passenger's side of his beat-up Silverado. He raced around the truck and sped into Main Street away from their pursuer. The noise of the streets had died since the sun had set, but he knew as soon as Jake arrived the place would be humming again with the commotion.

His gaze whipped back and forth between Addie and the road in front of him as he tried to assess her injuries. She was conscious, but he was worried she had a concussion. He cursed himself for not getting to her sooner. He should have seen it coming. He'd been warned by Butch and Karen, after all.

The faint headlights in the rearview mirror let him know this guy wasn't going to give up easily. As they exited the business district into the rural area surrounding the town, he jerked the wheel to the left in a quick decision, and Addie's barely conscious body fell into the door. He hadn't had time to buckle her in, and he doubted she was capable of doing it herself.

He drove for about a quarter of a mile before he found the hunting trail he was looking for and swung in, parking just far enough into the trees to be completely invisible from the road and cut the engine.

With heavy breaths, he released his white-knuckled hands from the steering wheel and clenched and relaxed his fists as he turned to Addie.

"Hey, stay with me, Addie." He grabbed the top part of her arm with one hand and cupped her face with the other. The left side of her head was turning an angry purple that he could see even in the muted moonlight.

She stirred and mumbled, "Declan?"

"I'm here. You're gonna be all right, Addie. Just hang on until I can get you to a doctor."

He pulled his cell from his pocket and dialed Jake again, leaving a voicemail with an update.

He turned back to Addie after ending the call, and she seemed more animated. "It's all right. You're safe now. I'm not going to let him get you. I need to know how badly you're hurt." Her shoulders eased down a fraction, and she took deeper, longer breaths.

"I...I don't think I'm hurt too bad." She cradled the left side of her head in her hand and squeezed her eyes closed. "My head hurts worse than anything, but things seem to be getting a little clearer."

"I think you may have a concussion. Do you feel sick?"

She shook her head slowly. "No, I did for a second, but I'm okay now." He would have to check her pupils, as soon as it was safe to use a light.

Suddenly, his hand holding her arm felt heavy. He looked down at the wound in his abdomen that he had almost forgotten about. He had been coddling her, but maybe he was the one in shock. He made a conscious effort to control his breathing and peeled his bloody shirt away from the wound and over his head.

A loud gasp from Adeline let him know she hadn't realized he was injured. "You're hurt. Oh no, what do I do? I'm so sorry."

A small smile crept across his lips, and the movement felt foreign. He looked up at her to find her gazing at his side and the blood running rivers over his torso. She was even cuter when she was flustered. It was then that she noticed the blood covering her own clothes from where he had carried her against his body.

"Just relax. I'll be fine. It's not the worst wound I've had." He watched her take in the scattered scars across his abdomen, chest, and shoulders. The aftermath of a life of fighting doesn't look pretty.

He used his teeth to tear a few strips from around the bottom of the shirt and pressed the remaining balled-up cloth to the wound as he tied the strips around his body to hold it in place.

Gritting his teeth, he lifted his hips with a groan to twist and tie the strap around his body, which was slowing down from the loss of blood.

"One thing you can do to help is get my phone and call Tyler. The number is in my contacts."

She grabbed the phone from the cup holder between them and squinted as she scanned the contacts. "Tyler Hart?"

"Yeah, that's the one. I can talk to him if you can get him on the phone." He finished the knot holding the makeshift bandage in place.

She hit the call button and handed over the phone. His breaths were ragged at this point, and the weight on his chest was getting heavier.

"Hey, man." Tyler always answered his phone before the third ring. It was an instinct from living a life on call for patients.

"Hate to crash your party, but I've got a situation here. I know you're off the clock, but can you stitch me up? And I've got someone else with me who needs to be checked for a concussion."

"Of course. Meet me at the clinic."

"Be there in five." The call ended before he could say anything else. Tyler was a doctor and could always be counted on to fix someone up, no matter what.

He turned to Addie who was staring at him as if she were waiting for instruction. "I think the coast is clear now. You ready to move?"

"Where are we going? Are you sure you're okay to drive?" she questioned.

His hands settled on the steering wheel again as the consideration in her voice lifted him a fraction of an inch. It was stupid of him to think she was concerned about him in any capacity above natural human sympathy. He had cut off all forms of emotional attachments years ago, before all the loss, before the Army. Still, he couldn't help wishing a woman like her could care for him one day. She had been attacked not half an hour ago and was more worried about him than herself. She was even more stunning in the moonlight.

He wasn't the pairing type. At least he didn't think so anyway. How could he know when the most recent part of his life had revolved around combat and survival? His mind hadn't been wired for female companionship for years now.

Declan tried to convey a sense of professionalism as he said, "Tyler is a doctor. He'll check us out at the clinic. I'll make it. Just keep talking to me so I stay more alert. I'm losing a lot of blood."

He was sure he'd never asked someone to make conversation before. This was really a first. He hadn't felt any of the usual discomfort the entire time they had been together. The only thing registering with him right now was relief. The feeling was so deep it was like he had been drowning, but now he was above the water again.

"Why were you still at the salon tonight? I thought surely you were long gone."

Her timid voice cut him to the bone. He was sure her ex-boyfriend had caused this hesitation in her, and anger boiled inside his gut.

"I decided to stick around for a minute." She had landed on the part he didn't know if he was supposed to reveal. How long should he keep his conversation with the Jacksons from her?

She bit her lower lip and frowned. "Why?"

Here goes nothing. "Well, I was watching you..."

"What?" The pitch of her voice went markedly higher, and she hugged the passenger side door.

"Wait till you get the whole story." He risked a glance at her with a calmness he hoped she would adopt, but she just stared at him, her adrenaline still piqued.

"I told you I ran into Butch and Karen today. Well, they mentioned the problem you're having with an ex-boyfriend and asked me to stop by and check on you. It was innocent, really. They were just concerned for your safety, and they knew I would help them out." He wrung the steering wheel back and forth in his hands as he drove. "I underestimated your situation. Letting him get that close to you was *not* part of the plan." His voice grew softer with the confession. At what point today had he actually formed a plan?

He scrubbed a hand over his bearded jaw. He couldn't look at her right now. His shame was too heavy.

When she didn't respond, he risked another look her way. Her mouth hung slightly open, and she was staring at him. "Okay, that's news to me."

"You're not mad, are you?" He really hoped he hadn't broken some kind of trust just now.

"No, I understand why they asked you to look after me, and I trust them completely. It turns out telling you my secret saved my life, so I'm grateful."

Moments passed in silence before she spoke again. "I knew he would come after me. I just thought I had more time. Silly me, I underestimated him too."

She paused for a fraction of a heartbeat and the volume of her voice was raised when she resumed. "Stupid. How was I so stupid when I knew this couldn't last? I lulled myself into a false sense of security in this quiet little town and completely forgot about the devil I was running from." She spoke fast then hung her head and cradled it in her hands.

"Hey, hey, none of that. I'm hearing some self-blame and you need to cut that out. You had every right to run, and it's not your fault he's a monster. Every bit of the blame for this goes on him. You hear me?" He really hoped Jake had gotten the guy tonight. He hoped the slimeball got what was coming to him after what he did to Addie.

She looked up at him like she was seeing him for the first time. He turned away from her to focus his attention on the road before he forgot himself. She was beautiful even covered in dirt and blood.

"What's his name?" He was too invested now. He had to know.

"Jason Broussard."

In the midst of his growing interest in Addie, he knew that name was going to be hard to forget. She said the name without a hint of emotion behind it. He couldn't imagine what that relationship had been like for her.

The miles passed in silence for a time before she said, "So, what do you do for a living now that you're not in the Army?"

"I'm doing some construction work around town with my friend, Dakota. When I get an extra second, I'm trying to keep up what's left of my grandparents' farm." He didn't know what kind of power she had over him, but he had never carried on a conversation with anyone so easily before.

"You're just a knight in shining armor on the side? I bet Santa always brings you plenty of Christmas presents." She gave a stuttered chuckle that told him she was trying to keep it together.

He was stunned to silence with a goofy grin on his face. "She makes jokes."

"Just trying to distract you, Boy Scout. Are all of those scars from the Army?"

She was stepping into deep waters now, and it was becoming increasingly difficult to share. "Most of them. Some were just teenage stupidity."

"Do you miss it?"

"Miss what?"

"The Army."

That was a loaded question. Sure, he missed the thrill of a mission, but he was lucky that he had so much to do to keep him busy here at home. He would have withered up and died if he'd had to succumb to a desk job. Building and working the farm was long hours and exhausting days, but he was used to the toiling. When he was forced to sit for hours, he felt like a caged animal.

But another part of him was happy to sever the ties of that responsibility. After watching two people he had come to respect die in the line of duty, he was ready to step back and hope no one else he cared for was taken from him anytime soon.

"Sometimes I miss it, but I've made my peace with leaving."

"You want to tell me about your family?"

Deeper waters. Too deep. Thankfully, they were close to the clinic now.

He huffed a deep breath and began. "I don't have much of any family. My mom died when I was eighteen. I don't know where my dad is anymore. I had my grandparents, but they're gone now. When I joined the Army, I never had a problem with deployments or missions. I went, tried my best to survive, finished the mission, and started over. Lather, rinse, repeat. That's a good summary of my adult life."

"Hmm." He could hear the wheels in her head turning in that one small noise.

"What's that supposed to mean?"

"I lost my parents when I was eighteen too." She gave him an appraising side glance. "Maybe we're not so different."

Deep waters again. He was definitely out of his element, and this woman had him on a lifeboat out at sea in less than an hour. For reasons he couldn't explain, the idea of her being alone caused him to have conflicting feelings.

He was equal parts angry, saddened, and comforted. He was angry that a woman as young as Adeline had been forced to endure the heartbreak of losing not one, but both of her parents.

He was saddened because he wanted nothing more than to comfort her when that was the last thing he knew how to do.

Lastly, the selfish part of him was comforted because maybe he was seeing someone else who knew exactly how he felt. He was no stranger to loneliness, and somehow sharing the feeling with someone else eradicated some of the sting.

Part of him was thankful to see the sign for the clinic. This woman was shaking him up, and he needed time to get his act together.

 CHAPTER FIVE

Adeline

They pulled into the parking lot of a dark clinic on the eastern side of town, and he cut the engine. A white SUV and a black pickup truck were also parked in the lot.

She hadn't meant to pry into some part of his life he didn't want to talk about. She wasn't particularly savvy at banter, so she had pulled from the first thing that came to her mind: his scars and his family.

Scars are reminders of the past. Even if it's over and done with, the past is a part of everyone. Now that she knew about his family history, she could see it was a sore subject too. She hoped she hadn't made him feel uncomfortable.

Declan opened the driver's side door and promptly fell to the ground in a heap, letting out a quick "Oof."

Shocked into action, she was out of the truck and crouched over him in no time. "Good grief. Are you all right? Declan?"

When his only response was a grunt, she launched herself from the ground toward the clinic to find Tyler. She burst through the door into an empty waiting area. She located a door and found herself in a hallway standing face to face with a tall, intimidating man.

"Please tell me you're Tyler. Declan collapsed in the parking lot and needs your help," she spat out in a rush and pointed to the open door behind her.

"I'm Ian. Tyler's brother," the man said in a deep voice. He gave her a stern look as he grabbed her shoulders and relocated her out of his way before running for the door.

She stood stunned in the empty hallway wondering why her heart was pounding so hard for the fate of a stranger. Sure he was a handsome, mysterious, Good Samaritan, but the fact that he was injured had her throat constricting like someone was physically strangling her. She could almost feel the hands around her neck. *Please, God, please let him be all right.*

The two men entered the hallway a few moments later. Declan's arm was draped over Ian's shoulders, and she realized the two enormous men took up the entire space. She ducked into the doorway of an open clinic room as they passed her.

Ian towered above her like a skyscraper. He was as thick as an oak tree, and his footfalls were deafening in his steel-toe boots. She watched him turn and kick open a door that was ajar, and she followed.

She entered the room behind the men as Ian helped Declan lie back on the table. Within moments, another man entered the room behind her. He was tall, like Ian, but where Ian was bulky and built to withstand a natural disaster, this man was trim and fit.

"How'd you get yourself into this mess, Dec?"

"It's no big deal." Declan halfheartedly shook the man's hand and gestured to her. "Tyler. Ian. This is Adeline Rhodes."

Tyler shook her hand and smiled brightly. "Nice to meet you, Adeline." He looked to be in his early thirties. If his welcome was any indication, his bedside manner was excellent. He assessed her quickly and asked, "Are you injured too?"

"I'm fine for now. I think Declan is first priority."

Just as Tyler turned back to tend to Declan's wound, another large man appeared in the doorway. The clinic room was too small for him to fit inside, so she pushed her way through the room to stand next to the doorway.

"Got the supplies you wanted, boss."

Tyler turned to wash his hands in the small sink in the corner of the room. "Thanks, Brian."

The man, whom she assumed was Brian, had naturally tan skin, light-brown hair, and chocolate colored eyes creating a dark, physical contrast to his upbeat tone. He laid the medical supplies on the desk and shook Declan's hand.

"How did this happen?" Ian's sharp tone broke her out of her shock. When she didn't answer immediately, he turned and gave her an impatient look, waiting for a response.

"My ex-boyfriend attacked me, and he saved me." She pointed to Declan just as he tried to lift his head.

"Easy. Just relax and let me work," Tyler told Declan.

She decided she probably hadn't given a very helpful explanation of Declan's injury. "He was stabbed while they were fighting, but then he had to carry me to his truck right after because we were being chased and I was hurt." She hung her head and started to bite her fingernails before realizing they were covered in dirt. She felt tremendous guilt for his injury.

Sarcasm dripped from Ian's words as he spat, "Good to know. Probably a dirty knife too."

Tyler turned to chastise his brother. "Get out of here and let me work."

Ian rubbed a hand over his bald head and pushed past her out of the room. Tyler seemed to calm a bit more and assured her, "All I can do is clean it, stitch him, and give him some antibiotics. He'll be perfectly fine."

Declan's voice was strained and raspy with pain as he spoke to Brian. "Take a look at Addie. She may have a concussion."

Brian looked her way for the first time with a friendly smile and motioned for her to follow him. "You can come with me. I don't think you wanna see this."

He led her out of the room and into another office a few doors down. "I'm Brian, Dec's friend. I'm much more fun and better looking, in case you haven't noticed." He gestured to a chair across from the desk. "Have a seat."

She laughed and sat in the chair he had indicated. "I'm Adeline, but you can call me Addie. Thank you for all of this. I'm scared, but Declan seems to know how to handle a crazy situation." She paused and considered who she was speaking with. "He's kind of... reserved."

"Reserved is one way to put it. He's just a loner. Don't take it personally." He smiled and squatted in front of her, placing both hands on her face as he assessed her bruising. His dark-brown eyes looked straight into hers and he said, "I don't think you have a concussion, but if you feel sick or disoriented, you need to tell Dec so he can call Tyler."

She nodded. "Thank you. You've taken really good care of me."

"No problem. Dec is gonna be fine. You can breathe now."

She let the air out of her lungs that she didn't know she had been holding, and her breath shook as a lump formed in her throat. Maybe this was the shock that Declan had mentioned. "I—I... This is all my fault." She couldn't keep it in now. She felt the tears welling in her eyes, and she wished she was anywhere but here in front of this stranger. He probably thought she was as weak as a pansy in a hail storm.

"Whoa there. No need for tears. Dec's gonna be fine." She wiped the lone tear from her cheek and looked into his honest eyes, seeing that he truly believed what he was telling her. He gave her a slow smile that eased her worries. "Everything is gonna be fine. Declan is made of tougher stuff than you know. I've known him my whole life, and he has definitely seen worse."

She sniffed. "It's just that he's a complete stranger who risked so much to help me. I owe him so much for what he's done for me."

Brian gave a short but bellowing laugh. "That ain't the way we work around here, missy. Dec doesn't help people to get something for himself. It's the way he's wired. He couldn't stop helping people if he tried, and I guarantee you he doesn't expect a thing in return. His reward is knowing you're all right."

She stared at him through tear-soaked eyelashes and smiled. "So he really is a hero? I thought that was just my addled brain playing tricks on me."

Brian stood with a knowing grin on his face. "Yeah, you can definitely say he's a hero." She could see a secret in his eyes as he held out his hand to help her up. "Let's go check on the patient."

They stepped back into the clinic room just as Tyler was removing his blood-soaked gloves. Ian had returned and seemed to be in a silent version of the same foul mood as before.

Tyler helped Declan to a sitting position as Brian asked, "How's he doin'?"

"Better by the minute. He just lost a fair amount of blood, but he will recover quickly."

Ian said, "Jake should be here any minute. He wants to get the story. Anything like this that goes down is definitely his business."

Just as he finished speaking, another man entered the room. He was tall and lean, but obviously fit with short, brown hair and the sweetest face she had ever seen on a man. He had a dreamy, handsome quality that would have made her want to pinch his cheeks if his huge biceps weren't peeking out from under his short sleeves. "Truer words were never spoken. How's Declan?"

"Fine, but I think he needs to rest before you interrogate him. She was there too, so you might want to talk to her first." Ian pointed at Addie, and she felt the weight of their stares.

The newcomer extended his hand to her and said in a friendly voice, "Jake Sims. Pleasure to meet you. I'm a Cherokee County deputy, and Declan's friend."

She accepted his hand. "I'm Adeline Rhodes. Declan saved me when I was attacked earlier."

"Yeah, he called me when he figured out what was going on. I'm sorry I didn't make it in time to help you."

Declan's gravelly voice came from behind Ian, "I'm injured, not dead. I can talk." He jerked his head up in greeting to Jake. "Good to see ya, Five-Oh."

"Been awhile, son. Like the beard. Nice touch." Jake reached out to forcefully shake Declan's hand, and she noticed he gave a controlled wince. Sometimes men didn't know their own strength.

"Thanks, man. You get that guy?" Declan asked.

Jake's lips formed a tight line. "Sorry, Dec. I got there as fast as I could, but there wasn't any sign of him. I called Helen to let her know what happened and that she needed to meet me there and lock up the salon. We took a look around, and she said everything seemed to be untouched. She sent Adeline's purse with me."

"Thank you so much." Addie cupped her hands over her mouth. She had been so wrapped up in the things happening tonight that she realized she hadn't locked up at the salon.

"No problem."

Declan and Addie went straight into the story of what happened. Jake stood with his arms crossed over his chest and hung on every word, only stopping them to ask questions from time to time. After the story had been told by Declan, Jake turned to Addie. "So, you know this guy? Jason. He's a threat to you, obviously. What do you want to do about it?"

"I—I don't know."

Declan cocked his head to the side and stared at her with his glassy eyes as if she were a puzzle. She was sure her cheeks were red with a blush. He was still shirtless and his jean clad legs hung off the table. She was definitely intimidated by his intense attention. "I've been thinking on it, but I haven't come up with a concrete plan. I'm open to ideas," Declan added.

"What do you mean? You think I need a restraining order or something?" She stared at each of them in turn.

Jake replied, "It's called a Family Violence Protective Order, but it serves the same purpose."

"But he's not my boyfriend anymore."

Jake gave a curt shake of his head. "It's still considered domestic violence."

"How—how do I get that order?"

Jake kept his militant stance. "You file for it with the court, but it isn't a quick process. In my experience, those who believe themselves to be above the law won't be stopped by a piece of paper that tells them not to do something."

"Then what are you saying?"

Declan turned to Jake. "She already agreed to help me work on my grandparents' house. We'll be spending a good bit of time together. I can keep an eye out for her. If you can send someone to drive by the salon where she works every now and then, we shouldn't have a problem from Jason anymore."

She looked at Declan and couldn't believe what he was saying. "I appreciate everything you did for me. I'm truly grateful, but I need to take care of myself. I don't want to be a bother." She couldn't put him out more than she already had tonight.

Declan looked tired and gave a muted sigh. "We're only trying to help you. I think between us and a few people we know, we can truly catch this guy and get you out from under his thumb. You'll never be free until we get to the bottom of this. We're not the kind of guys that are going to be able to turn our heads knowing you're in danger and we could help. Besides, we all know Butch and Karen. We can't just ignore your problem."

Brian piped up, "She knows Butch and Karen?"

"Yeah, they're my aunt and uncle. I'm staying with them for a while."

"How did I not know this? Why didn't Karen mention she had a beautiful niece?" Brian crossed his arms over his chest, and she smiled. Did this guy have a serious bone in his body?

"Because she's running from a controlling ex-boyfriend, in case you didn't hear the story she just told. The last thing she needs is a date with a man-child." Declan shrugged his friend off and turned back to her. "What do you think?"

Declan gave her a wordless plea, and her walls crumbled. He was looking into her soul, and she could feel his need to protect her in every fiber of her being. Without breaking eye contact with him, she conceded. "All right. Thank you."

Jake kept his head down and tapped his fingers on the desk he was leaning on as he spoke. "How do you feel about drawing him out?"

She looked at him and realized he was completely serious. Her chest constricted instantly just as Declan's booming "No!" filled the room.

There was silence for a moment while Declan stared a hole through Jake who still hadn't looked up. "No, absolutely not. Not an option. We can't put her in danger. We know what he's capable of, and I'm not willing to accept the consequences of our failure."

Jake pushed off the desk and leveled a serious glare on Declan. "You know I'm thinking about what's best for her. We can flush him out, and we have enough eyes to make sure we spot him first. I'll have the sheriff's department on it, and we can get Dakota and Marcus to help watch. We can make sure she is seen at the most popular places around town, and Jason will have boots on the ground who will find her soon enough. We can actually find him. I looked in on this guy. He's slick. He's got a long list of warrants, not including the one coming from the charges she's gonna press tonight. This is one man our department wants off the streets." Jake's persuasive voice was calming her, but Declan seemed unaffected by anything he said.

Addie piped up, "Oh no, I don't know if I want to press charges. That'll just make him angrier."

Declan's face was turning red, but Jake was the one who said, "That's up to you, but you can take some time to think about it."

Declan wasn't giving up on this one. "I'm not willing to let her prance around town like bait!" Jake threw his hands in the air and turned away from him.

Ian seemed to be warming up to the idea. "What if she has a sort of bodyguard? Not necessarily a bodyguard, but someone who is always with her to protect her. We can still catch Jason before he strikes, and both sides win."

Brian draped his arm over her shoulder as he added, "You should let me take you out on a couple of dates. That would really make this guy mad, and I can promise you a good time." He winked at her, and she gave a joking laugh.

If looks could kill, Declan was shooting daggers at Brian. "No way."

"Why not?" Brian asked in a joking, whiny voice as his arm dropped from her shoulder.

"If anyone is pretending to date her, it'll be me." As if he realized the strangeness of his remark, he turned to her and his features softened. "Butch and Karen already asked me to keep an eye on you. That is, if you're okay with that plan. I could take you out to different places around town like we planned. We'll go places where we know there will be a lot of people to see us, and I'll be right beside you in case he gets any ideas."

Declan's blue eyes were glued on Addie, and the silence lingered in the room. She could see the wheels turning in his head, and surely she was imagining the spark in his eyes.

How did she feel about all this? Could she really trust these strangers to keep her safe? One of them was a deputy and one of them had straight-up saved her life. Yet, all of them had come through in a heartbeat for her in some way or another tonight.

Finally, Declan spoke. "How do you feel about that?"

She looked at them all in turn but settled on Declan and expelled a heavy breath. "You really think this is a good idea? You would pretend to be my boyfriend to protect me?"

Ian quipped, "You could always keep hiding out. That sounds like a great way to live life." It seemed like the only thing Ian understood was sarcasm.

Brian answered in his stead. "Of course, it's a good idea. I thought of it."

"It was a collaborative effort, don't you think?" Jake chimed in.

"Whatever. You can pick up your participation trophy at the door." Brian waved him off.

Declan still hadn't broken eye contact with her. "I think it's better than any of the ideas I've come up with, and I've been thinking about this since you were attacked."

That was good enough for her. She had no idea why, but she trusted him to have her best interest at heart. "Okay, I'm in."

Brian clapped loudly once and started for the door. "All right, let's do this, ladies."

Ian rubbed his bald head again—it was definitely a nervous tic—and pushed off the wall he had been leaning on. "Let's get y'all home." He left the room and Jake followed close behind.

When she and Declan were the only ones left in the room, she went to his side to help him as he pushed off the exam table with a grunt. He tugged a T-shirt Brian had given him over his head and put his baseball cap back on.

She could feel the blood rushing to her cheeks and stepped toward the door. She was supposed to be going on dates with this man, but they weren't really dates. The lines of their relationship were already murky. This plan had just taken a turn she hadn't considered. "I, um, this is all a little fast." She was floundering, and she knew it.

He staggered as he made his way across the room to her and put both hands on the tops of her arms. This was the first time she had been able to really look at him closely. His shoulders were wide enough to cast a shadow over her as he stood in front of her, and his posture was militant despite his wound. His brown hair was short beneath his cap, and his beard had a dark spot that she assumed was blood. He was taller than her, and she had to look up into his eyes as he slowly but firmly rubbed his hands up and down her arms.

"Please let me help you. I couldn't sleep at night if you said no."

He was laying on the charm, and he knew what he was doing to her. Her heart constricted at his kindness. "Thank you." Her voice cracked on the last word. She tried her best to pull the tears back in, but they had already decided to break free.

He gently ran the pad of his thumb over the tear on her cheek, and she gave a quiet gasp. His gaze held hers, and she was lost in the blue depths of his eyes. Surely, this shade of blue was the most beautiful she had ever encountered.

His tone changed to serious, and his voice dropped even lower. "I know this is a lot to take in, but I promise you I will do everything in my power to keep you safe." He slowly wrapped his arms around her body and held her. The smell of blood and dirt didn't mask the masculine scent that tingled in her nose, and it made her heart flutter. It was the primal smell of protection, and it had been a long time since she felt safe. She felt like he was holding on to her for dear life, and she wrapped her arms around him. The feeling of being cloaked in safety was overwhelming. She knew without a doubt this man was going to buy her freedom, whatever the price may be.

She couldn't think of a time in her life when a man other than Jason had held her. In fact, she couldn't remember a sensual touch from Jason. This was probably the most intimate physical moment she had experienced. Jason hadn't hugged her like this.

She felt Declan smell her hair just before he broke the connection and nodded to the door. "We should get going." He wrapped his arm around her shoulders and led her out the door. "It's getting late. Let's get you home. Butch and Karen are probably worried sick."

 CHAPTER SIX

Declan

What in the world had he been thinking? Why had he hugged her like that? Sure, she was upset about being attacked and what this meant for her future, but he had never known how to comfort someone who was hurting before. It was as if he couldn't help himself. He had let himself be drawn to her like a sailor to a siren. He couldn't have stopped himself any more than he could stop the wind from blowing.

He wasn't a soft man, emotionally or physically. He'd been hardened by loss and war for too long to be an adequate companion to someone as fragile and sweet as Adeline. He wasn't sure he was capable of attachment, and she deserved someone who could cherish her when all he could think about was how he would never be enough for her and the people who mattered the most in his life always seemed to leave him. He didn't know how to emotionally empower a woman like Addie who needed building up in so many ways after being torn down. Talking to women hadn't been a skill he had spent any time enhancing in his life.

Still, their connection had started off with a bang, and it had been natural. Maybe that was cause for hope. His mind had been overloaded with the instinct to protect her, and she seemed like a safe place to rest his head.

The surprising part was that she had hugged him back. She completed the connection and raised the stakes each time she accepted him, flaws and all. Had she melted into him because she wanted to or because he had been her only support at the time? He felt more than he ever had for a woman, and the foreign emotions made him uneasy.

After convincing Ian that he and Addie could make it home on their own, Jake walked them to the parking lot.

"I'm calling in for a drive-by service on your house until further notice, Adeline. I'll have someone check in with you at least twice a day. You said you're staying with the Jacksons?" He wasn't asking her permission. The matter was settled.

"Yes. Thank you, Deputy Sims. I really appreciate it."

"Call me Jake." Jake's attention toward Addie had Declan itching to have her to himself again.

Something was different. He had never been jealous a moment in his life, until Addie came along. The fact that she was a free woman with the power to choose to turn her back on him brought back the powerless feelings from childhood. He wasn't a stranger to watching people leave.

"Well, you can call me Addie."

Declan shook hands with Jake to dispel the nervousness creeping up on him. "Thanks, man. I'm gonna call Dakota and let him know what happened tonight. We're swamped at work, but he'll have to understand that this is important." Not that he was complaining. The longer it took to find Jason, the longer he would get to wine and dine Addie. Spending extended amounts of time with her could turn out to be a blessing or a curse.

"Let it sit 'till morning. He can't do anything about it tonight. After that meeting he had today, you might not want to poke the beast."

Declan scratched his head. "Yeah, he had his hands full today, and he wasn't in the best mood when we talked earlier."

"I think he ended up at the races with Marcus tonight anyway," Jake added.

"Gotcha. I'll give him some space. You sure he's all right? He's not going off the deep end again?"

Jake shook his head. "Nah, he's past that I think. Well, as far past it as he'll ever be."

"That's good news." He nodded and clapped his friend on the shoulder, ready to get out of there. "See you, Five-Oh." He was thankful Jake wasn't a Chatty Cathy because his mind was still stuck on Addie standing beside him.

Seriously, he couldn't get her out of his head. She was there to stay. *Snap out of it!* He shook his head to dislodge the thoughts.

Jake gave them a knowing smile as he turned and walked to his car. "See you two later."

They didn't speak until Jake's car was out of sight and the silence of the parking lot begged to be obliterated.

"I guess it's time to get you home." He took one step toward the beat-up work truck before stumbling and catching himself on the hood.

"I think I should drive," Addie said as she reached to support him.

She was right. He didn't feel comfortable driving right now, especially not with her in the truck. "You sure you're up for that?"

"I'll manage." Thankfully, the old truck was automatic. He didn't know if she could drive a stick shift or not.

"I'll have to see if Butch or Karen can take me to get her car in the morning. I've been driving it since I got here."

"I can take you by there tomorrow. I'm supposed to be picking you up anyway, remember?" The parking lot was pitch black, and he wished he could see her reaction.

"That would be great. I forgot all about helping you tomorrow. I'm glad I'll have something to keep my mind busy."

He regained his footing and helped her into the truck, realizing she hadn't complained about her bruises at all. She was tougher than she looked, and he was sure she was strong enough to tackle this mess and still come out on top. He couldn't help the proud smile he felt covering his face as he closed her door and walked to the passenger's side.

A thought occurred to him as they drove through the dark streets of Carson. "I don't think it's a good idea for you to go to work for a few days. You'll most likely be sore and bruised. People will ask questions. It may be best to give it until next week so you can heal."

In truth, he also had selfish reasons for asking her to stay out of work for a while. He wanted her safe, but he might get to spend even more time with her this way. It just happened to benefit him too, and he couldn't hate that.

She sighed, and his heart went out to her. "I can't afford to miss much. I'm just getting started. I've never had a job, and I'm trying to pay Butch and Karen back for school."

"You're in school?" What if she was younger than he had assumed?

"I started cosmetology school a few weeks ago. Jason would never let me have a job, so I'm not trained for anything. I never even went to college."

The more he heard about her time with Jason, the more his anger boiled. What kind of man didn't *let* his girlfriend go to college or have a job?

"Did you say he wouldn't let you have a job?" Maybe he had misheard. The idea was so archaic.

"He was more than a little controlling." She kept her eyes focused on the road ahead, but he wished she would look at him. What could he possibly say to let her know that what Jason had done to her wasn't acceptable? That not all men were controlling and aggressive?

She gently chewed her bottom lip in the midst of her worry. "I guess it would be rude and sketchy if I had to keep putting off answering those questions all day about my bruises."

"You don't need to worry about money right now. I'll make us breakfast and take you to lunch and dinner. Then we can go out on the town and show you off. I'm your new boyfriend, remember? You pick all the places." He paused before adding, "When you're feeling up to it, of course."

He didn't want to push her. He was pretty sure that's what Jason had done. Besides, he was sure she wouldn't be jumping into the limelight for the same reason she wasn't running back to work.

He could just make out her smile glowing in the yellow-tinged street lights, and he knew that smile would bring him to his knees.

"I wouldn't mind a day off I guess. And I can still go to school I think. There aren't many other people in my classes, and I can't afford to fall behind." She turned to him but quickly shifted her focus back to the road. "How is your side? Is it bad?" The concern in her voice was thick as he adjusted his posture in the seat as best he could with the least amount of pain.

"I'm fine. He didn't hit any internal organs. I think it didn't so much stab in as it slashed across the surface. It's not as bad as it looks." The bandage Tyler had put over the stitches was more to keep her from seeing it. It wasn't pretty. "Brian said he would drop off my antibiotics in the morning."

"You have some amazing friends, you know that? They all stepped up and helped us tonight without a second thought."

"And they'll keep doing it too. I was away for eight years with the Army, and I've only been back for a few months. They've been hounding me like crazy to hang out, and I've been kinda lazy about getting back to them." The guilt hit him again. "We've always had each other's backs. That won't ever change."

He almost didn't hear her whisper, "You're lucky to have them."

CHAPTER SEVEN

Adeline

They pulled up to the curb in front of Karen and Butch's house about ten minutes later, and she hesitated before getting out of the truck.

"What are we going to tell Karen and Butch? I know we're basically putting on a show with this whole fake relationship thing, but I don't keep any secrets from them." She was almost pleading, and she hoped he could understand the extent of what she was asking. They had been there for her through everything that had happened with Jason so far, and she trusted them completely. The trust that she shared with them was rare. She didn't have friends she could count on like Declan did.

He reached across the seat to her and placed his hand on top of hers. It still shocked her how his touch could calm her. "I think we should be honest with them. I've known Karen and Butch my whole life. They'll understand, and they'll certainly want to help you." He opened the door and stepped out.

"You've known them your whole life?" It amazed her how everyone knew each other in this small town.

"Yeah, they went to church with my grandparents, and Ms. Jackson was my third grade teacher."

Now that was just funny. She could imagine a little rambunctious eight-year-old Declan being scolded by her Aunt Karen, and she couldn't contain her giggles. "You're kidding! That's the best thing I've heard all day."

They entered the house to find Butch sitting on the couch watching television in a heather gray Georgia Bulldogs T-shirt and dark green-and-blue plaid lounge pants. He wore thin-framed glasses, and his bald head was shining in the light from the lamp beside him on the end table.

"Hey, Addie. Whoa, Declan, what happened to you?" He made his way to his feet and gave Declan a hearty handshake. "Are you all right?" Her uncle took in Declan's disheveled appearance. His hair was tousled and a slight bruise was forming on his cheekbone from the one punch Jason snuck in.

In a more hurried gesture, he turned to Addie, immediately searching her for injuries. "Baby girl, are you all right?"

She shook her head and immediately regretted it as her brain felt like it was tumbling around inside her skull. "I'm all right, Uncle Butch."

"Addie and I ran into a bit of trouble tonight. That's why I'm here. I wanted to make sure she made it home safely." Declan's tone was calm, but it did nothing to alleviate Butch's concern.

Karen walked in about the time Butch was beginning his questioning, and zeroed in on Addie's bruised face. Her light-brown hair streaked with gray was pulled back into a short ponytail, and she looked ready for bed. She had no doubt in her mind that her aunt and uncle had waited up for her, and she felt a sting of remorse. She hated to worry them, especially since the threat of Jason had been looming in the forefront of their minds for a while now. They had all been dreading this day, and the worry on her aunt's face was like a knife in her heart. The poor woman didn't deserve this.

"Baby what happened? I've been calling you." The panic in her voice echoed her bulging eyes. Karen grabbed her face and started examining it from every angle.

"I'm fine. He came for me tonight, and Declan saved me." There was no question as to who *he* was. "I'll tell you everything, but I need to get cleaned up." She looked down at her bloodstained shirt and Karen whimpered.

Addie hurried to assure her aunt. "It's not—"

Declan interrupted, "It's mine, Mrs. Jackson. I'm all right, but Addie will have some bruising for a while. I'm sorry I didn't get to her sooner."

Her Aunt Karen reluctantly released her and turned to Declan. "Oh, you sweet man." Her arms were around him in a heartbeat, and Addie held her breath as she waited to see the discomfort on his face from either the physical interaction or the fresh wound on his abdomen. She released the breath in a rush when it never came. Maybe he was too distracted by the awful things that had happened tonight. "Thank you for being there. We owe you a great debt."

"Not at all, Mrs. Jackson. I'm just glad you said something to me this morning." He released Karen and looked at Addie over the older woman's head. "Addie and I have decided to spend a little more time together." His interest shifted to the floor as he stated, "We want Jason to think I'm her new boyfriend, and maybe he will leave her alone when he realizes he'll have to go through me." He turned back to Karen with a reassuring smile.

Karen's brows inched higher, and she gave a mischievous smile. "That sounds like a wonderful idea." Karen turned back to her and let her eyes run over the bruises and scratches again. "I'll help you clean and bandage some of these cuts after you get your shower."

Declan shook Butch's hand and grabbed the doorknob. "It was nice seeing y'all again. I'll be back in the morning around 7:00 to pick you up, Addie."

She knew it was late and he should be going, but a part of her felt the loss of the comfort he had given her tonight. Seeing him leaving was harder than she expected.

"Thank you for everything, Declan." Her voice was soft in her sudden nervousness. "See you in the morning."

"Good night." His blue eyes held hers for a moment longer before he turned and left.

Addie didn't move as she felt the remnants of her energy seep from her body in his absence. Her shoulders sagged and her head hung low as she turned to her aunt and uncle. "I'm really sorry I wasn't able to call tonight. I hate that I kept you worrying."

Karen nudged her toward the hallway. "Don't bother another minute about it. We're just glad you're home safe."

She closed the bedroom door behind her and took a moment to breathe in the smell of her aunt and uncle's home. The scent of vanilla and sugar would always remind her of the Christmas holidays she had spent here over the years. Those were the best times of her life.

This place was like a sanctuary for her, and she loved being here. Living here felt more like a fancy vacation than a new home. It wasn't a particularly large or lavish house, but the relaxing qualities of this place made her feel like she was living in a five-star resort.

She took in the sparse things throughout the room that belonged to her and wondered if she would ever have a real home again—a place with roots and staying power. Would she ever get on her feet and find her place?

She felt a renewed scorn toward Jason for what he had done to her tonight, but she couldn't completely blame him for the situation she was in. She should have paid better attention. She should have gotten away from him sooner, before he descended so far into this hateful madness. She had a responsibility as a grown woman to protect herself.

Jason was a dangerous man who was out for her blood, but she shouldn't have let him get so close. He had slithered his way into every aspect of her life, and she had practically sat back and let him. She had been too soft, and now she was paying for being so negligent in the past.

She had been too accepting of him in her efforts to be tolerant and not seem ungrateful. She hadn't trusted him, and she had given him too much power over her, and now he was coming to collect.

Why was her wariness and anxiety mounting now? A capable, dedicated man had pledged to protect her and help her until further notice. She was lucky. No, she was blessed. It was clear God had kept his hand on her tonight. In the midst of all the evil attacking her, God was always there.

To be honest, she felt excited about the idea of spending time with Declan. He was quickly captivating her thoughts, even amongst the mess that Jason had brought into her life, but she couldn't help but fear she was setting herself up to become blinded in the same way she had been with Jason. If she had learned anything from this, it should be to keep her guard up.

She moved in front of a decorative mirror in her bedroom and her heart sank as she took in her reflection. The bruises were new and hadn't grown into their full color yet, but they looked nasty just the same.

She eased her body onto the bed and wondered how long her life would be in flux.

She had been with Jason since she was seventeen. She was twenty-four now, and in all the years they had been together, she had never once even thought about another man. Not because she had been happy or content in their relationship, but because he had driven a fear into her head so solid that she was afraid to open the door to let even the smallest amount of light in. Any infraction was dangerous with him, and she had walked on eggshells around him. She hadn't known what he was capable of at the time, and she hadn't wanted to find out.

Then she had broken his trust when she left him without a word, and tonight she had suffered a small portion of his wrath. She couldn't let her fear win the battle this time. She would keep pushing those memories of his fingers digging into her skull into the deepest depths of her memory until they were nothing. She would snuff the memories out in darkness until they didn't own her or control her anymore. She could only have room in her life for freedom and happiness now. Anything else would be unacceptable. This was her time to shine and take charge of her own life.

Now she was free, and the fear of looking at another man had waned, but not disappeared. She couldn't think of a reason why she shouldn't let herself open up to Declan. She was free to do as she pleased, and he was going to be pretending to date her anyway.

The problem would have bitten her if it had been a snake. How was she going to know if he was putting on a show or if he was really interested in her? She didn't know how to date, and she certainly didn't know all the games people play when they try to woo each other.

She was definitely going to fail at this. Carve it in stone. She was going to drive him away with the baggage she carried. It's not like she knew how to put herself out there anyway. She had spent her whole life trying to be invisible, and Jason had spent the last six years hiding her away from the world.

Now, here comes Declan ready to parade her to the world on his arm. She didn't know what to think of it, but there was no way she could deny the connection she felt to him.

No. She wouldn't let her doubts rule her anymore. Declan had been good to her, and she didn't want to live the rest of her life as a wallflower because she was afraid of getting hurt. What was that saying? *Better to have loved and lost than never loved at all.*

She urged her body to get up and take a shower before bed. She needed the best shower of her life to wash the memory of Jason's filthy hands from her in that alley tonight.

As the near scalding water pelted her skin in what should have been the most cleansing shower of her life, she couldn't help but feel cold and dirty. She scrubbed her skin until the abrasions hurt, but she still felt the dirt. It was embedded in her skin.

The water was washing away the physical dirt and blood from the night's injustice, but the naked truth was that the shower that should have comforted her was exposing her isolation.

After her shower, she changed into a tank top and comfy shorts for bed.

Karen entered the room as she rubbed a towel over her wet hair, and they sat on the bed together.

"I'm so sorry this is happening to you. You deserve this least of all people." Her aunt gently ran her hand up and down her back the way she used to do when she was a little girl. Karen may have been her father's sister, but she was more like a mother to her than an aunt. Karen reminded her of Mom all the time, but she caused a calming in Addie instead of sadness like her mother's memory.

"Do I? I let him control me and practically own me for years. I should have gotten away from him before things got this far." She hated spreading her problems into the lives of others.

"Oh, don't give me that." Her aunt's tone was harsh and clipped. "This isn't your fault, and you know it. That monster has a lot of problems in his head, and he is just mistakenly under the impression that you're one of them." Karen pulled her close and rested her temple against Adeline's.

"We knew this was a possibility, but I'm glad Declan was there to help you tonight. I'm glad he's volunteered to help you going forward too, now that we know the worst is coming. I can't imagine a better man to entrust with your safety."

Addie stuck her clean fingernail between her teeth for a moment before catching herself. "He's been very good to me, and I want to trust him too. It's just… hard now… to know who to trust."

She hesitated. How could she say what she was thinking? She shouldn't be letting herself have hope. Looking down at her hands, she finally whispered, "He's so different from Jason."

Karen grabbed her shoulders to gain her full attention. "Hun, that's not saying much, but you've gotta know that you deserve so much more than Jason. I understand that he is all you've known of a relationship, but that is nothing like a healthy relationship will be when you find the right one." Karen's eyes were full of sadness, and Addie couldn't have loved her more in this moment for all the care and support she showed.

"A man should care about you in every way and never make you feel like you are less than wonderful. A good relationship is built on reciprocity and mutual respect. A true man will never stifle you like Jason did. I saw Declan look at you earlier, and I think he sees the strong, intelligent, capable woman that I see when I look at you. Don't be afraid to trust new people and to move on to better things because you've been hurt in the past. You're only holding yourself back. It's not fair to Declan or anyone in your life to be hindered by Jason's mistakes. You learned a lifetime's worth of lessons from that relationship. Use that information going forward to know when love is right."

Karen rubbed her hands over Addie's tangled hair. "Let me brush your hair."

Addie crossed her legs beneath her and reveled in the gentle tug of the brush gliding through her wet hair.

"I don't know if hanging out with Declan will keep Jason away." The fear she had been hiding sprang into the air between them. "I'm just scared."

"I know Declan and his friends, and they will do everything they can to keep you safe. They are all very smart and capable men. I wouldn't be surprised if this Jason problem is resolved sooner than we think."

Karen set the brush down and kissed her cheek. "Good night. I love you."

"I love you too."

Addie turned off the lights and slipped into bed and thought about her aunt's advice. Her relationship with Jason had been a study in how a relationship would fail. Jason had been ice: cold, frigid, and unforgiving. Declan was his antithesis. He was fire: hot, selfless, and unstoppable. Generally speaking, fire was more destructive. Fire, like Declan, had the power to hurt her in ways that Jason's ice-cold heart could never touch.

Ice left you uncomfortable, while fire left you scarred and changed forever.

Change was scary, but it was becoming a constant part of her life. She could either move with the changes and choose the best paths going forward, or she could let the past eat her alive.

There was no going back now. She would tackle any obstacle that came at her and trust in God to lead her in the right direction.

CHAPTER EIGHT

Declan

Declan wasn't sure why, but he was nervous when he pulled into his driveway with Addie the next morning. The insecurities probably came from the fact that he had lived here his whole life and never brought a woman home.

His German Shepherd shot out from behind the house full of excited barking before either of them made a move to get out of the truck. Hopefully, Addie wasn't afraid of dogs.

"Who is that?" she asked. He relaxed a fraction and smiled when he heard the excitement in her voice.

"That's Reaper. He's been with me since I came home." They exited the truck and she walked around to meet him and Reaper on the other side. She didn't make a move to pet him, but she was bouncing on her toes in excitement, while Reaper backed up against Declan to assess her.

"You can pet him. He's a guard dog, but he takes cues from me. He already knows you're not a threat."

She bent at the waist to pet him and whispered endearments in his ears as he wiggled into her affections. Within seconds, she was laughing and gently wrestling with him in the yard like a kid. He had underestimated the ways that she could pull him in closer, and she kept surprising him.

"Okay, kids, it's time to come inside." He let out a deep chuckle as he called to them. It sounded strange to his ears. He couldn't remember the last time he had laughed.

Addie and Reaper bounded up behind him as he threw his keys in a bowl beside the door and stepped to the side to let her enter ahead of him. Reaper snaked his way around their legs and into the house. The sky was turning a threatening shade of gray and thunder rolled in the distance.

"I know German Shepherds aren't usually house dogs, but he sleeps inside from time to time." He wasn't ready to tell her the reason just yet. Reaper was more than a guard dog. He'd come to be more like a service dog. Reaper knew how to wake him up and settle him if he had a nightmare or a flashback to some of the more life-threatening times in the Army.

"That's good." He watched her raise her fingers to her mouth then drop them.

"Do you think he should stay inside when you're gone for now? One of the goals of this fake relationship is for Jason to see us together. He'll figure out where I'm spending my time sooner or later, and I would hate for him to take it out on Reaper." She hugged herself and looked away from him as Reaper danced in circles on his bed in the living area before plopping down in a settled heap.

He had already thought of the same thing. "I'd planned to keep him inside a little more until this dies down. Don't worry. Make yourself comfortable." He was nervous and had no idea what he was doing. This was virgin territory, and he realized it mattered to him what she thought of his home.

"Wow. Um, this is..." She trailed off as if she wished she could backtrack on her sentence.

"It's what?"

"Just not the bachelor pad I expected. Are you married?" she asked tentatively.

"Definitely not." He couldn't help the huff that came with his response. "This is the house I grew up in, and I've been slowly renovating since I came home. I build houses, so I put in a little work on my own in my spare time. Also, the Army sort of drilled the need for a clean home base into my head. Mess stresses me out."

"Can you show me some of your work?"

"Sure, come this way." He led her down the hallway to a bedroom and opened the door for her to step in. Standing in the doorway, he watched her observe the room. She turned a complete three-sixty, taking in everything from the plush beige carpet to the sea foam green walls and the tray ceiling before she stepped out of her sandals and dug her toes into the plush carpet. Everything in the room had the crisp, clean lines of a new renovation.

"I just finished remodeling this room. It was my bedroom growing up."

Having someone in his personal space was new to him, but welcoming Addie into his home this morning hadn't been as difficult as he had expected. He was almost relaxed.

"What did it look like before you remodeled?" Her curiosity was cute in all the right ways, and he suddenly wished he had all the answers for her.

"Imagine blue walls, baseball posters, and sports trophies. It was a mess, so I started my work here. I didn't really spend much time in this room growing up anyway, so I thought it was time to gut it." He shrugged and he gave her a glimpse of a lazy side smile.

"Why didn't you spend time here?" Her brows drew together in concern.

"Mom couldn't keep me indoors during the day. I'm more comfortable outside, so I was out the door as soon as my feet hit the floor in the mornings. When I got a little older, I didn't even want to come inside at night. My friends and I slept outside more times than not growing up."

He made a lazy circle around the room, keeping distance between them as she inspected every inch of the space.

"Sometimes, I felt the need to stay home, but I just wasn't ever here enough to have a space that I wanted to make my own." He couldn't bring himself to tell her why he had been needed here sometimes. He hadn't felt the urge to talk about home, well... ever.

He rubbed his neck and asked, "You hungry? I planned to make breakfast."

When she turned to him, the vulnerability on her face was like a punch to the gut. "I hate that I've caused you so much trouble."

"It's no problem at all. I *want* to help you anyway I can." He stepped toward her and rubbed a calloused hand up her arm. She gave a soft sigh, and he could feel her relax into him just a little. He relaxed, knowing he wasn't the only one affected.

"We're gonna fight this together, and then you'll be free. No one will control you or own you, especially not Jason. You've been full of smiles this morning, and it looks good on you. We're going to win that back for you all the time. Think about the reward. Freedom."

This was starting to sound like a motivational speech.

"Have you ever done anything like this before?" she blurted.

"No. Not really, but don't worry. Everything is going to work out."

He had put his life on the line many times to protect his co-workers, but never had he felt the fear of losing so harshly. He didn't know why he would be willing to go above and beyond anything he had ever done for her, but he knew in the deepest part of his soul that he would do anything for Addie.

He turned to step away, but it was harder than he expected. The fear was still heavy on her face, and he wanted to comfort her, stay with her, and just be with her. He wanted to be close to her.

"I'll get breakfast started."

"I'll help." Her voice sounded as sweet as honey tastes, and something about it was familiar, though he couldn't imagine why.

Had he ever cooked a meal with someone? The thought hit him hard that the only person he had shared a kitchen with was his mother. *Don't think about her now. You're past that.*

He definitely felt something for Addie, but he had no idea how to even begin with a woman as broken down by a man as she had been. In light of her last relationship, he felt like he could easily mess everything up.

CHAPTER NINE

Adeline

Addie loved breakfast food, and the smell of cooking bacon had her stomach growling. Declan laid out food for a full breakfast this morning, and her anticipation was mounting as she flipped the sizzling bacon. She couldn't think of a better way to get motivated to work than making breakfast.

She usually helped Karen cook breakfast in the mornings, but she had spent years making every meal alone. Jason never cooked for her. She had even cooked the meals when she had been sick.

Her body still ached from the attack. Waking up this morning had been worse than she expected, and playing around with Reaper in the yard had caused a few winces. Her muscles and bruises protested as she carried the plate of bacon to the table.

She was starting to realize that some places have the potential to feel like home, and some just don't. Her aunt and uncle's house had always felt like home, and her childhood house with her parents had been home. Jason's apartment had never felt safe to her, for whatever reason. She had lived there for years, but she had never relaxed enough to enjoy the place. It had felt like a prison more than anything else. Actually, it *had* been a prison, since she technically hadn't been allowed to leave without Jason's permission to go to the grocery store or on some other menial errand.

Declan had told her that she was welcome in his home and to make herself comfortable at his grandparents' house too. They planned to ride over and start on the cleanup after breakfast.

The small gesture of welcoming had meant more than he realized. He had immediately shared his world, his safe place, with her, making her feel at home for a little while.

She had been nervous today before she saw Declan, but once they were in the truck together, she couldn't remember why she had been timid.

She turned to watch Declan work as he scraped the eggs onto a serving platter. He was facing away from her in front of the stove, wearing Army green shorts and a black T-shirt. Reaper sat begging at his feet, and she couldn't help thinking that the image was beautiful. She had never described a man as beautiful before. Maybe the way he interacted with her had something to do with her views. He was so effortlessly himself that she hated he had trouble talking to people sometimes. He had so much to offer, and she wanted him to always know his worth. Granted, his issues communicating didn't seem to be a lack of confidence. He had done nothing but try to assure her he would protect her.

He gave her a playful wink as he moved the food to the table. Would she ever get used to the lighthearted way he acted with her? She had heard of people who described butterflies in their stomach when they were with someone they cared for, but she had never experienced it herself until now.

She made herself useful and set the table. He pulled her chair out for her to sit, and she felt like a queen. She sat down and took in the mouthwatering smell of the spread in front of her. "This looks amazing. Thanks again for breakfast."

He took his seat across the table and passed the bowl of scrambled eggs to her before taking any for himself. The fact that he served her first didn't go unnoticed. She couldn't think of a time when Jason had put her first, yet Declan had done so since the moment they met.

He told her about his plans for his grandparents' house while they ate. It was startling how different he was when they were alone. He didn't fidget or get tongue-tied like he had with Libby at the salon. She listened, but she couldn't push past how much he had done for her in the short time they had known each other.

Her face turned warm and a lump formed in her throat. What was happening to her? Surely she wasn't getting mushy at the breakfast table from some sweet sentiment he hadn't even realized he had made.

When he looked up at her, she tried to hide what she was thinking, but she had never been good at that. She was as easy to read as a book, always wearing her thoughts on her sleeve.

"Did I say something that upset you?" he asked, and she was embarrassed to have caught his attention.

"Oh no, I'm fine." She allowed herself a deep breath before continuing. "I'm just so thankful for all that you've done for me. I don't know where I would be right now without you." That was the truth. She would probably be dead if Declan hadn't come to her aid when he had. She had no doubt Jason was capable of bloodshed. She had seen it in his eyes, as clearly as she saw the care in Declan's eyes right now. The contrast was startling.

She stood to let him know that she didn't want to continue this conversation anymore. "Are you finished with your plate?"

He looked down at the table as if he had forgotten where they were, and he ran a hand over his bearded cheek. "Yeah."

She quickly grabbed both empty plates and made her way to the sink. She felt him standing behind her as she washed and rinsed the dishes, but didn't turn around. She was afraid her body would betray her and give in to the safe haven he could provide her when she really just wanted to cry on his shoulder again. She wasn't going to be that woman anymore. She could be stronger, and her mind was made up that she would try her best not to succumb to her weak moments.

He gently ran his hands up her arms, and she felt the strength to turn to him. He smelled like spice and woods.

"I don't want you to hide what you're thinking from me." His voice was full of honesty and concern. He was telling her she could be herself with him without judgment or fear of getting hurt like in her past.

"I'm not hiding."

She let her gaze travel down his torso and linger where his stitches lay beneath his shirt. "Does it hurt?" she said as she allowed only the tips of her fingers to touch the area.

"Not a bit. I don't even need the pain meds Tyler prescribed."

He pulled her close to him as his head bent to her. She was taller than average for a woman, but he still towered over her. Their noses were almost touching. She could feel the heat from his breath and smell the bitter aroma of coffee. "Don't worry about it anymore. I promise I'm fine. It was worth it to keep you safe, you know that, right?"

Her heart beat faster as they drew closer. "How could that be worth it? You could have been hurt worse or killed." She was letting her fears out to play now. The truth was that she had been secretly terrified of what Jason could do to either of them if they weren't careful.

"Oh, ye of little faith." He gave her a carefree smile. "My pride is the only thing that's injured. I could take that guy any day. I won't spend my nights worrying about that, and you shouldn't either."

He tilted his head slightly to the right side and dug his fingers into her arms. His tone was serious and strained, while his gaze held hers captive. "You are beautiful, Addie. You're so beautiful and strong."

She couldn't breathe. Her heart hammered. She had been driving herself crazy since they met wondering if he felt something the way that she did. Now that the moment had come, she was frozen like a deer in headlights.

Her hands slowly drifted up to land on his wrists that held her arms. When she finally found her voice, it was a soft plea that whispered, "Declan…"

A loud bang came from the front door and she jolted in his arms. She panted, unsure if it was from the sudden scare or the tension between Declan and herself.

He gave a furious, low growl before he reluctantly released her. "Brian must have brought Dakota with him."

A tan, black-haired giant of a man stomped into the kitchen. He was wearing an orange vest with reflective yellow stripes over a sweaty white T-shirt, dark jeans, and tan work boots as he pointed at them accusingly. "I know what the two of you were doing. No need to act innocent."

"Adeline, this is Dakota. He doesn't have any home training," Declan said in a deadpan voice. "Ever thought of calling first?" he questioned.

Brian was right behind Dakota and hit him in the shoulder when he passed. "Leave them alone, Dakota."

She moved slightly toward Dakota and said, "It's nice to meet you." She didn't know what else to say. It was clear he wasn't interested in pleasantries.

Dakota gave her a half nod and sat at the table without looking at her. "I'm up to speed on what's going on here. I'll let you off the hook as much as I can, but work is busy and I need you back on your feet at the job site as soon as the weather clears up. I couldn't even run the Bobcat for Jim this morning when he called me because of this rain." He was clearly talking to Declan. He was finished with her.

Brian leaned over and whispered in her ear, "Don't let him bother you. Dakota isn't ready to grow up, and he has a slight aversion to women. It's a long story."

"I got it. I'll be back in the morning." She could see the tension in Declan's stance as he spoke. Was he on edge because his friends were here or because they had been interrupted?

She heard Dakota mumble something that sounded like "whatever" as he grabbed a fork and dug into their breakfast leftovers straight off the serving trays.

It was clear that Dakota wasn't her biggest fan, but hopefully he would warm up to her soon, because she liked his no-nonsense attitude. She thought about the way Declan and his friends seemed to work together like a well-oiled machine. Every man knew his part, and together they made a great team.

What had been happening between her and Declan before his friends had barged in? She knew he would have kissed her had they not been interrupted. She wasn't sure if she could resist him if he had, and furthermore, she knew she didn't want to.

He was swinging into her life like a wrecking ball, and she couldn't find the need to protect herself from him. She knew the odds of a relationship actually working out these days. So was the downfall worth this elated feeling he gave her, this burning ache in her chest?

She wasn't imagining the attraction between the two of them. He truly seemed to care about her safety. Well, she knew what it was like when someone didn't care about her, and that was what she had to compare this to—a broken, toxic relationship.

Jason wouldn't be happy if he found out she was seeing someone else. If he saw them out together now, he wouldn't know the relationship wasn't as real as it seemed. He would never be able to sit back and watch her with someone else, and she knew he wouldn't let her live after seeing the fury in him during the attack at the salon. If she ever wanted to move on, she was going to have to do everything in her power to bring Jason to justice.

She hadn't known he was dealing drugs until the day she decided to leave him. That bit of information had spurred her out the door quicker than she thought possible after living a stagnant life for so long. Not only was he breaking the law, but he had put her in danger of being implicated in his crimes. He was a danger to her and whoever else crossed his path.

In that moment, she decided to flaunt herself in public with Declan with everything she had in order to draw Jason out of the shadows and into the trap they were setting for him. She wouldn't be able to live with herself until it was over. She would grow stronger, and she would be a force to be reckoned with the next time she met Jason.

This time, she planned to win her freedom.

CHAPTER TEN

Declan

He couldn't believe Dakota's nerve. His friends bursting into his house wasn't an uncommon occurrence, but insulting Addie wasn't acceptable. He understood Dakota's problem with women, as much as his friend understood his introversion, but he had to draw a line.

A phone began ringing, and Addie reached for her back pocket. "I'm sorry. This is my boss. I'll be out on the porch if you need me."

After Addie left the room, he gave Dakota his attention. "What's your problem?" He was tired of these games, and his friend had chosen the wrong time to bring his attitude for a visit. Something had been happening between Addie and himself, but it felt like he would never get to the bottom of it at this rate.

"You know, I had a friend named Declan once. Have you seen him?" Dakota gave him a daring look.

"What are you trying to say? Just spit it out."

"I'm saying you met her yesterday, and you're cuddled up in the kitchen with breakfast the next day. The man I know can't form a full sentence in front of any woman between the ages of twenty and forty. What gives?"

He didn't want to have to explain this to his friend. "She's just different. She's easier to be around."

Dakota turned away from him and stuck his fork into the plate of scrambled eggs. "I just don't get it."

Declan pushed away from the counter and ran an agitated hand through his hair. "I don't have to explain myself to you. Why do you even care? I said I'll be at work tomorrow."

"I'm just trying to figure out how much you've really changed in eight years. Is your problem getting better or is your problem that you're ready to settle down and she's someone who could really be good for you?"

He knew the answer, but he was afraid to say what he was thinking out loud. He ran his hand through his hair and sighed. "You and I both know that I am who I am. I haven't changed since we were kids, and I don't know if I will." He paced the floor and tried to gather his thoughts. "Addie is different. She's good and strong and sweet, and I want to help her. I'm still getting used to her being around, but it hasn't been so bad having her here. I know this adjustment will take a while, but I like where things are going. I'm just taking it one step at a time."

Brian bit into an apple where he had crouched down to pet Reaper. "Yeah, hanging out with Addie sounds tough. I'll expect all the awful details later, including how horrible it is getting to take her out on 'dates' all the time." The sarcasm brought Declan out of his slump and reminded him that he really was living a charmed life. Brian always knew how to keep tensions at bay.

Turning back to Dakota, he said, "The more I find out about what she has been through, the more uneasy I feel about this guy coming after her. I mean, he attacked her last night with a knife. You don't pull a knife on someone for anything other than torture or a quiet death. I can't get it out of my head, Kota. I have a feeling he won't just give up on her."

Dakota gave him a side glare. "You know I've got your back. I saw those bruises on her face, and I'm taking it seriously. My advice is that you need to help her, but also let her in. Let her in so much that she breaks down all those walls you've held up your whole life. The two of you could be good for each other." Dakota put the fork down and crossed his arms over his chest. "I know I'm the last person to be giving advice about letting someone in, but you need it. You need someone, and if you aren't going to let your friends in, then it should be someone like Adeline. Just don't get distracted. Keeping this guy off her back is priority number one."

Declan heard his friend loud and clear. Dakota wasn't a fan of losing people he cared about, and Declan packed up and left years ago only to come home a little more hardened and a little more distant.

"You're right. I'm gonna try my best for her and hope something works out right in the meantime."

Dakota pushed his chair away from the table with a screech. "Sounds like a plan. I've gotta get to work. I got rained out at the job site about half an hour ago, but Mom needs some work done on her bathroom."

He shook hands with Dakota as Brian threw a white paper bag at him. "Tyler sent these. He said the pain meds are optional, but the antibiotics are nonnegotiable."

"Thanks, man."

Addie walked back into the room with a smile on her face. Seeing her gave him that burst of happiness he still wasn't used to. He turned back to Dakota. "Hey, did I hear you still play poker on Wednesdays?"

Dakota looked at Brian like a cat looks at a mouse. "You better believe we do. Brian is on a twelve week losing streak."

"I think it's rigged. There is no way I'm not winning at least once," Brian huffed.

"I want in this week. We can play here," Declan said, looking at Addie. "You know how to play poker?"

She shook her head. "I never tried."

Oh, this would be fun. "You want to play with us on Wednesday night? I can teach you how to play. We play Texas Hold 'em and Five Card."

"That sounds great, but I don't have any money to play around with. Especially if I'm new and bound to lose."

Brian had his arm draped over her shoulders in no time. "Listen here. You can do anything you set your mind to, sweet cheeks. And don't worry about the money. We just play with chips."

Declan gave a single booming laugh. "Still?"

"Old habits die hard. Plus, it's better for my bank account," Brian quipped.

That was the truth. Declan and his friends had been playing poker for fifteen years, and Brian still didn't know how to win.

Declan turned to Addie and explained. "When we were in high school, six of us played poker every Wednesday night. Me, Kota, Brian, Ian, Jake, and Marcus. We didn't have jobs yet, so we were playing for keeps with our parents' money. Needless to say, that didn't sit well when our parents were always crying, 'Where's my money?' They finally wised up and started grounding all of us only on Wednesday nights. After that, we had to promise not to play for money so we could hang out on Wednesdays."

Addie laughed and turned to Brian. "Is this a joke?"

"No, and I'm probably the only one who will never vote going back to playing for money. I couldn't afford to hang out with these cheaters if we did."

"What do you say, Adeline? Are you in?" Dakota was asking, and Declan knew that meant his friend was serious about the advice he had given him a moment ago.

"Sure. It sounds like fun."

Dakota nodded his acceptance. "Ian gets off work at seven. We usually get started around eight."

Brian yelled a sing-song good-bye to Addie as he and Dakota walked out, leaving Declan alone again with Addie. She averted her gaze from him, but a smile lingered on her lips. "I'll help clean up the kitchen, and then we can head over to your grandparents' house."

"Thanks for agreeing to poker night." He rubbed the back of his neck and tried not to look at her as he cleared the table. "I've been shutting those guys out for a while now, but I think it's time to…" How could he say he wanted to let people in, specifically her, without sounding so forward? "Maybe it's time to work on changing what I'm doing with my life. I've been alone for so long, it was just easier to stay that way. You've put the buzz in my head that spending time with someone else can be fun."

"Really? You like spending time with me?"

He turned to her and shrugged. "What's not to like?"

Maybe Dakota was right. Addie could be the key to fusing his old life and his new one. She had certainly done a good job so far. He had been a lot less jaded before his life had been turned upside down after high school. Part of that was youthful innocence, but part of it was a product of the circumstances he had faced.

The bruises on her face shown through the makeup she had used to hide them, but she was still stunning. Without the bruises, she wouldn't need the makeup. "You know, you didn't need to try to cover up the bruises today. It's just us."

She didn't look up from the dish she was rinsing and raised one shoulder. "I thought I might need to start trying to figure out the best way to cover them. My boss said she would let me off until I was healed, but that could be a while. She said once the injury isn't as noticeable, if I wanted to work in the back office with her, I could get a few hours in stocking."

"That's good." They finished up in the kitchen and he looked at her as she dried her hands on a kitchen towel. They decided to pack sandwiches for lunch and dinner. She wasn't ready to be seen in public with bruises on her face, if it could be avoided.

Her blue eyes were shining, and her brown hair was pulled into a high ponytail showcasing a few bruises on her neck he hadn't noticed the night before. He had to look away before his anger boiled thinking about what she had been through.

"You ready to get to work?" The clock on the microwave read almost 9:30 as he grabbed the sandwich bags.

"Lead the way."

Chapter Eleven

Adeline

Declan lived on a farm just outside of the business district in Carson. His house sat unimposing against rolling green hills and scattered barns sectioned off with wooden posted barbed wire fences.

The farm was wrapped on three sides by a dense tree line that ran along the western side of his house, along the back forty of the property, and met the road again about a half a mile away.

They bounced along a worn, muddy path through the open field toward the back of the property. The rain had dwindled from a downpour to a sprinkle, but they were expecting another round of heavy thunderstorms after noon.

While Declan's house was about one hundred feet from the road, his grandparents had lived in the shadows of the trees lining the back of the property. The house wasn't even visible from the road due to the rolling hills.

"Your farm is beautiful. We didn't have farms like this in New Orleans. I didn't get outside of the city much." Truthfully, she hadn't been outside of the city since before she lived with Jason. She just couldn't remember much about her time with her parents. It seemed like another life, and one that didn't belong to her.

"Thanks. I've always been partial to this place myself, but I'm biased." Declan's wrist hung loosely over the steering wheel as they jostled along in a red Ford pickup truck.

She looked to the back seat where they had packed deconstructed boxes, packing tape, and markers for sorting the items, and he told her it was safe to assume his grandparents already had some cleaning supplies they could use.

"So you have two trucks." It was just an observation, but she wondered how he had acquired two in the few months since leaving the Army.

"This one was mine that I left with my grandfather during my first deployment. I couldn't really take it overseas. I was in Germany for a few years and didn't have a use for it. The older truck was my grandfather's. He left it and everything else they owned to me when they died."

In the spirit of keeping the mood light, she didn't ask more about his family. "What kind of farm is this anyway?" She looked out the window and spotted a pond nestled behind the terrace they had just capped.

"We raised livestock and chickens mostly. A lot of this land was for baling hay. I thought about keeping the hay business going, but I didn't have the time this year. I planted one patch in the far front pasture, and it'll need some attention soon."

"What happened to the animals?"

"Pop sold them off before he died. We had talked about it, and he knew I couldn't get back in time to care for them if something happened to him suddenly. The last few years were a big change for him. He was eighty-five years old when he died, but he didn't quit until his body forced him to."

"He sounds like a good man. You speak highly of him."

"Of course, I loved them both a lot. They were the only grandparents I ever knew. My dad's folks aren't from around here, but they died when

I was young anyway. My dad's side of the family lived hard and died young as a general rule."

He mentioned his dad had left them, but she wondered if he was still alive. That was a question for another time.

They rode in silence for a minute as he let her take in the vast acres. "I always knew I would end up back here. I just needed to get away for a while. My grandparents were the only ones I was leaving when I went off to Basic, and they understood it. That doesn't mean they didn't miss me a lot."

A quaint, dirt-colored brick house came into view, and he parked beside it and shut the engine off. Nestled into the trees, Declan's grandparents' home reminded her of a cottage in a fairy tale.

"I loved my time in the Army. I know it was the right choice for me, and I was good at my job. But now I know I missed time with them I can't get back."

Now she understood a little more about why he needed a push to clean out his grandparents' house. She could imagine dealing with loss was complicated further by his inability to open up. Sometimes talking helped, but everyone handles grief differently. "I'm here if you need me. We can talk about it if you want, or

I'll let you have your space." She laid her hand over his and he turned to grasp it.

"Thanks. Just having you here is helping." They grabbed the packing supplies from the truck and she helped when he didn't have a free hand to unlock the side door. When she opened the door, she stepped aside for him to enter first.

"I'm glad I made one trip over here to clean out the food and turn off the A/C and gas after they died."

The place looked like someone could have been there just a few hours ago. The shades were closed, but a faint light filtered through the curtains into the living room. A modest tan couch divided the room into the gathering area and a designated pathway through the room to the kitchen.

The place hadn't been updated in decades, but it was clean and tidy. Knickknacks and picture frames covered every level surface. The dust-brown carpet was worn low in a path from the door to the kitchen across the room, and the morning sun shone in specks off the popcorn ceiling. A round mosaic hung on the wall beside the door that read "I may sleep in the house, but I live in the garden."

Declan dropped the boxes onto the couch. "I completely forgot how much stuff granny had in this house." He scanned the room with a daunted look on his face.

"We'll get through it. We just have to…" What was the plan for tackling this project? "Maybe divide and conquer? I'll clean and you can sort the stuff until I get more familiar around here."

He rubbed his beard as if he was thinking but didn't move to get started. "Yeah, I guess that's what we need to do." He dropped his hands to his sides and looked at her with a growing smile. "When all this is said and done, I still have to go through Pop's workshop out back. He was even worse about keeping everything he came across." He laughed at the enormity of the job in front of them. "I guess I need to ask some of my friends to help with that job. They'll want first dibs on the tools."

She stepped toward him and rubbed his arm in reassurance. "We'll get it done. There isn't a deadline I don't know about, is there?"

"You're right. We're not in a hurry." Declan let out a huff of breath. "I've already promised the furniture and any household necessities to my grandparents' church. They have a small building where they store decorations and stuff, and I figured they could keep it there for anyone who needs it. Every once in a while someone falls on hard times or some house fire or tornado levels a house and people need a fresh start."

His kindness knew no bounds. "That's very thoughtful of you, Declan. You could really help someone out by donating this stuff." The furniture might have been older, but it was in excellent shape.

"The miscellaneous stuff needs to be put in boxes of like items and labeled for the donation drop-off. Unless I run into someone who wants any of it, I'm planning to just donate it. I don't know if I'll find much use for anything here myself."

"Sounds like a plan. Where do you think I could find some cleaning supplies? We can start on this room together and work our way toward the back of the house." The whole structure was one level, and there didn't seem to be too many rooms. Maybe this wouldn't be as difficult as she first thought.

His voice fell as he confessed, "There's a basement."

Of course, there was a basement. This place was full of surprises. "We'll get through it. Let's get started."

They stopped for lunch a few hours later, but getting back to work was easier the second time. They fell into a system where she dusted each fragile figurine before handing it to him to be wrapped and packaged. When he didn't need her help, she worked on the floors, baseboards, ceiling fans, and blinds.

The picture frames all held some variation of his grandparents, his parents, and Declan. She had commented on some of the younger photos of him, and she could tell he was embarrassed by a few. She noted his father had only been present in two of the photos, and the ones that featured him were at least fifteen years old, judging from Declan's age.

She also noticed that his mother was stunningly beautiful. Many of the photos of his mother featured a larger than life teased and sprayed hair style, but her facial features were the parts that captivated Addie's attention. After remembering how vague Declan had been about his parents, she decided it was best to pack them up quick. They were shoved into a box he had marked *To Keep*.

They had worked through the entire living room by seven o'clock in the evening. She was sticky with sweat, and hairs had escaped her ponytail and clung to her forehead. She had wiped the back of her hand across her head once and winced. She had forgotten about her bruises.

Her body was protesting with sore muscles by the time the boxes that would fit had been loaded into the truck, and she was sure her comfortable bed was calling her name. There was work, and then there was *work*.

"I'm sorry it took so long today. I didn't mean to have you digging ditches on day one." Declan reached over and placed a hand over hers as he drove through the pasture back toward his house. She felt a surge of energy at the touch and remembered how well they had worked together today. Being with him was a breeze.

"It's fine. It wasn't so bad, and I feel fulfilled. We made a lot of progress today." She gripped his hand and smiled.

"We do make a pretty good team. Thanks for all your help. I don't think I would have ever even started this, if you hadn't agreed to help."

She let out a contented sigh. "I don't mind. I don't have much to do on my days off except study. I haven't made many friends here yet." She stretched her aching legs as far as she could in the cab of the truck.

"I'm sorry I worked you so hard. We'll do this in shorter shifts from now on."

She laughed. "Deal."

She helped him unload the boxes into a corner of his garage he had cleaned out before he dropped her off at Karen's car at the salon. Declan didn't say anything as he put the truck in park beside the sidewalk on Main Street. She thanked him for the ride, but he leaned toward her slowly. Her breathing slowed to match his progress, but he stopped when his face was only an inch from hers.

"I know we were working today, Addie, but I had a great time with you. Not many people would help me do this, and fewer people would have been able to sit in a room with me all day in silence without getting antsy. I can't thank you enough."

They hadn't actually worked in silence. Once she started humming along with her work, he had asked her to sing, and she had. The various songs she knew by heart had provided the soundtrack to their afternoon.

His fingers touched an unmarred spot on her cheek just below her bruise, and her breathing stopped completely. This was it. He was going to kiss her, messy hair and all.

When his lips touched hers, she breathed in a lungful of air that she hadn't been able to grasp before. He was breathing life into her, and she felt like everything was good and right with the world.

She had never had a more perfect kiss, but this was it. The kiss lasted only seconds, but they were powerful dots of time. She opened her eyes as he pulled away, but he was already jumping from the truck.

Her mind hadn't regained its control function as fast as his, and he was opening her door to extend a hand to her before she knew what he was doing. "Do you mind if I follow you back to Butch and Karen's? I would feel better if I saw for myself you made it home safe."

Her cheeks must have been a rosy shade of red, and she dropped her head with a smile to hide her nervousness. "Are you sure it isn't too much trouble?"

"Not at all. I'll pick you up from work on Wednesday for poker night, but I'll call you tomorrow if that's all right with you."

"Of course. Thank you again for the ride to pick up the car."

"Good night, Addie."

"Good night, Declan."

She got into her car feeling happiness flood her bones, warming her from the inside out. Pulling out onto Main Street, she touched her lips to feel the lingering tingle but didn't feel the urge to bite her nails.

She glanced into her rearview mirror and remembered the last time she had been looking back to see if a man followed her. When she left New Orleans, she had been terrified Jason would trail her, but tonight she drove in a cloud of contentment watching those headlights follow her home.

Chapter Twelve

Adeline

Declan picked her up at Butch and Karen's for breakfast before work on Wednesday morning and asked if he could pick her up from work before the poker game. He told her he had been asking his friends to drive by to check in on her when he couldn't do it himself, and he mentioned that Brian would be riding by sometime today. He gave her a quick kiss as he dropped her off at the salon and promised he would be back well before her shift was finished at 6:00PM.

For the last few days, Declan had been eager to drive her to work or school. He always arrived early to pick her up and escorted her through the parking lot. She told him it wasn't necessary, but he insisted. She had been borrowing Karen's car to drive to work these past few months, and she knew her aunt was growing tired of sitting at home without a means of getting around.

He had allowed his life to be consumed by her, and she always felt a stab of guilt thinking of how inconvenienced he must be by her intrusion in his life. She spent one day this week lounging in the back of his truck with her textbooks while he worked at a job site. The fact was he had allowed her to invade his life in the short time they had known each other. She mentioned to him that she felt like a bit of a burden, but he wouldn't hear of it. Even his friends were going out of their way to help her, but he assured her that they look after their own.

Still, she couldn't understand what that had to do with her. She was an outsider, a complete stranger before a week ago, and they had decided she was worthy of the inconvenience. She certainly hadn't done anything to earn their loyalty, but that didn't seem to matter to them. They saw her in her time of need and hadn't hesitated to move their lives around to help.

The immobilizing feeling of being watched began about halfway through her shift, and no matter how hard she tried to distract her mind from it, the gnawing feeling persisted.

She wasn't a stranger to this feeling of being hunted since coming to Carson. She had felt it numerous times before Jason had found her, but this was the first time she had felt the fear creep in since she had begun spending time with Declan. She had felt so safe and protected the last few days that her past fears had simply been forgotten.

She kept telling herself she was imagining things, but trusting her instincts felt like the smart thing to do. She pulled her cell phone from the back pocket of her jeans and contemplated texting Declan.

She was still rolling her phone around in her hand when Declan himself walked into the salon a few minutes later. His eyes immediately found hers, and he gave her a heart-stopping grin.

She realized that she had missed him in the few hours they had been apart and chastised herself for being so needy. But she couldn't help the natural need she felt to be near him. He set her at ease, and she silently wondered if it was the protection he provided or the feelings she couldn't help blossoming in her stomach. She was still so new to dating or relationships with anyone that she found she didn't always understand the emotions that came with spending time with someone.

"What's wrong?" She could hear the genuine concern in his voice.

"Am I that transparent?" she questioned.

"I like to think I can read you better than most." He gave her a playful wink.

She tucked her phone back into her pocket as she steadied herself.

"I got the feeling that someone was watching me today."

His smile fell, but she could see that he tried to compose himself for her sake. "You know it may have been me. I watch you like a hawk."

A hawk was a bird of prey, but she knew in her bones that Declan hadn't been the predator watching her.

"Maybe you're right." She hung her head, feeling foolish for exposing her weakness, and bit at her fingernails on instinct.

"Chin up, sweetheart." He casually lifted her chin with one finger. "Even if he is watching you, always remember that I'm watching you too. I'm always here, and I'll protect you. He'll have to go through me to get to you, and that would never happen." He sounded so sure of himself, and she was just as confident that Jason was no match for Declan.

"We need to stop by the grocery store on our way to the house to pick up some snacks for the poker game tonight."

"Okay." She was nervous about hanging out with all of his friends tonight, but she was trying to hide it.

He had a carefree attitude now, and his tone lightened. "They're gonna love you, Addie. These guys are as laid back as they come."

Well, that set her a little more at ease. She could feel the blood rushing to her cheeks. "But I've never played poker." Her confession was continually embarrassing.

"It's all right. We don't play too seriously, so it'll be easy for me to teach you as we go tonight. Just watch out for Brian. He's pretty competitive, and it doesn't help that he's awful and really wants to win. Don't be surprised if he cheats."

She couldn't help the laugh that escaped. Brian was becoming easier to like by the day, and she could imagine the jokester being a sore loser. "Maybe I'll win some points with him, since he won't be the worst player anymore," she said with a smile.

"Oh no, sweetheart, you'll be taking his chips by the end of the night, if I have anything to say about it."

They made a quick stop by the grocery store to grab chips, dip, pretzels, and beef jerky for the men and some granola clusters for her. The list didn't sound like much, but buying enough to satisfy six grown men was ridiculous. He even threw in some Oreos and milk for her when he remembered she had mentioned liking them before.

She noticed he hadn't picked up any alcohol. She had never been interested in drinking alcohol, but she had just assumed the men would be drinking tonight.

When she asked him about it, he explained that the guys would drink on occasion, but they never had alcohol around Dakota. Their friend had a problem with alcohol that had almost cost him his life a few years ago. Out of respect for his struggle, they always refrained from mentioning it while they were together.

Her respect for him grew exponentially, in light of his concern for his friend. Not many people would be so selfless, but it seemed all of their friends shared that trait.

Declan had begrudgingly exchanged pleasantries with a few people he knew in the store, and she noticed he fumbled his words when it came time to define their relationship and introduce her as his girlfriend. She wondered if someday he would introduce her as his *real* girlfriend and if he would feel more comfortable about it. She silently hoped that day would come, but she also knew that hoping for things to work out between two people who had the deck stacked against them wasn't smart. They hadn't known each other for very long, but she could see herself being happy this way.

On their drive to his house, Declan turned on the radio and a mainstream pop country song filled the cab. Her feet tapped to the beat without her consent. When the next song started, he turned to her and said, "Name that song. Bonus points if you can name the artist."

Now this was a game she could win. Music had been a form of expression when her identity had diminished to nothing. She could relate to the song lyrics and know that she wasn't alone. The melodious words calmed her and took her mind off things she shouldn't think about.

"You're on. What do I get if I win?" she asked in a devilish tone as she rubbed her hands together.

"Whatever you want, sweetheart."

She quickly recited the song title and artist before switching through the stations and naming all the other songs.

When she had circled back around to the original station, he slapped the steering wheel and laughed. "You're a musical encyclopedia. That's impressive."

"It's not so impressive when you realize I had nothing else to do for years."

She could see his struggle to ignore the reference to her isolation. "Well, winner, winner chicken dinner. What do you want for your victory?"

He watched her thinking for a moment before she asked, "Can I save it for later?"

"I feel like this is going to get me in trouble, but sure."

Jake and Brian were already at Declan's house by the time they arrived. They were in the front yard playing keep away from Reaper with a tennis ball. They both exchanged greetings with her and grabbed a few bags of snacks to carry inside.

The four of them milled around in the kitchen making small talk and joking around while picking at the assortment of snacks. Dakota came in a few minutes later, followed by a man she didn't know.

"Addie, this is Marcus," Declan said in introduction.

The dark-skinned stranger's lips didn't seem to smile, but his eyes connected with hers in a way that expressed greeting as he pushed his hand through his slightly shaggy black hair before extending his other to her for a handshake.

"Hi, I'm Addie. It's a pleasure to meet you."

He didn't respond as he shook her hand stiffly and gifted her a single nod of his head before sitting down in a seat at the small breakfast table in the kitchen. He seemed more quiet or reserved than openly unfriendly.

Shivers ran down her spine as Declan leaned close and placed his hand on the small of her back before whispering in her ear, "Marcus doesn't talk much, unless he knows you well. Don't take it personally." She watched Marcus for a moment as he did seem to hang around the outside of the circle observing intently. "He's good at reading people. He stays quiet until he figures you out."

By the time they had moved the snacks into the dining room to use the larger table for the game, Ian had arrived. Brian greeted him loudly, "Hey, man, what took so long? I thought you were wrapping things up when I left an hour ago."

"Last-minute wrench in the equation. Mindy ordered a huge shipment of the wrong siding today, and I had to correct the order." He ran his hands over his bald head then rested his fists on the table. "This is why I would rather just do it all myself."

"We've talked about this. You can't do it all anymore, so you have to delegate. There is a learning curve, but she'll get it one day," Brian assured him.

"Well, until then, my job is getting harder," Ian barked.

Jake walked in with the bowl of granola clutched to his chest and a stick of jerky in his free hand. "This girly crunchy stuff is good." He looked around for half a second and said, "We only have six chairs," before taking a huge bite of the jerky.

Addie looked around the room to see that while the dining room was big enough to house a six-seat table, it wasn't a large enough room to comfortably accommodate another chair.

Brian plopped down into a seat. "That's perfect. I've got a seat right here for you, Addie." He playfully gestured to his lap.

Declan had sat in the chair behind her, and she felt his strong hands grab her hips before he purposefully pulled her back into his lap.

"No way. She's sitting with me," Declan growled.

Still sitting on his lap, she turned to him with a smile on her face. His claiming had been much clearer this time than it had been earlier in the grocery store when he was scared to introduce her as his girlfriend. He didn't have to play games with anyone here.

"I am?" she challenged. Last she checked, she belonged to no one, but she needed to hear his reasoning for the sudden possessiveness.

He ran his hands over his face hard. "I didn't mean that. Of course, you can sit with Brian if you want."

She only deflated a little. He had misinterpreted her question, but only slightly. The lines of their relationship were still defined by the charade they were playing. Their feelings were confusing. What was real, and what was acting? He had laid a claim to her in front of his friends. She didn't take her eyes from his. He looked hurt, but she knew it was just his pride.

"I think I'll stay here. I'm pretty comfortable."

He relaxed but still didn't smile as he dug his fingers into her hips. His hands on her felt so right, and she didn't want him to let go.

She smiled as he rested his forehead against her arm.

"I hate Wednesday nights." Brian threw the deck of cards on the table in front of Declan. "You're first dealer."

Declan wrapped his arms around her to grab the deck of cards and began speaking low in her ear about the basics of the game while he shuffled the deck like a professional casino dealer. She tried to listen to his lesson, but she couldn't take her eyes off his skilled fingers.

"Let's get started, boys." Ian's loud voice pulled her from the secluded moment she shared with Declan.

Declan whispered in her ear again. "You ready, sweetheart?"

"As ready as I'll ever be. Let's play."

By midnight they were all getting more comfortable with each other and everyone communicated in loud voices and open-mouthed smiles. Everyone was having a blast, except Brian, who seemed to be the butt of all the jokes.

Declan had proven to be an amazing teacher, and they had played all of their hands together. He wanted her to make the plays after she got the hang of things, so he sat back and only gave feedback when she asked.

"It's beginner's luck! Next week, you're goin' down, missy!" Brian was sporting a smile as he pointed at her, pretending to be a sore loser.

"You don't stand a chance. She'll be getting extra lessons before our next game," Declan assured him as they made their way toward the door. Brian leaned in for a hug but settled for a one-arm side hug when Declan released a low rumble.

When Declan closed the door behind Brian, the last one to leave, he turned and leaned back against the door, giving her a relaxed look again.

"I thought they'd never leave," he finally said.

"Me either." She laughed, knowing he was joking. It was clear he had enjoyed himself tonight. "I guess it's my turn to leave too. Do you mind if I use your bathroom first?" It had been a long day of work at the salon, then the poker game had lasted well into the night. She was exhausted but filled with excitement at the fun night she had been a part of with new people.

"Not at all."

She stepped into the bathroom and locked the door behind her. Being alone still triggered memories of being trapped in Jason's apartment, but the noise Declan made as he milled around in the kitchen calmed her. He was a big man, and subtlety wasn't his strong suit. It was as if her body knew she was safe as long as he was near, and her heart rate stepped down gradually.

She took her time in the bathroom freshening up and pulling herself back together. She wanted to relish these last few minutes in the comfort of Declan's shadow before she had to go home. Her bruises were healing slowly, but they didn't look quite as angry anymore.

When she stepped into the kitchen a few minutes later, she realized Declan was nowhere in sight and the house was silent. She felt a prickling in the back of her neck but forced herself to remain calm until she could locate him. Surely, he hadn't left. Reaper was still in the same position as earlier and raised his head at her entrance. Seeing only Addie, he settled back into his bed and stilled.

As she reached the kitchen, she turned to look out the cracked French doors and spotted him on the back deck. He was reclined in a patio chair with his feet crossed on the porch railing in front of him. The black T-shirt he wore made him hard to make out against the onyx sky. He was a picture of tranquility, with his head tilted back looking up at the vast open sky, and she suddenly wished she knew what he was thinking.

This was the moment she stepped out of her comfort zone and pursued something she wanted. She could do that now, and she had sat timid on the sidelines for way too long.

She knew the risk she was taking. The lines of their relationship hadn't been drawn, but they felt real just the same. Still, something propelled her forward. He was drawing her to him like a magnet. She had no reason to resist and many reasons to give in.

Chapter Thirteen

Declan

Addie had been a dream to watch tonight. She had laughed and joked with his friends as if they had known each other for years. Her carefree happiness made the air lighter, and he was sure a goofy smile had been plastered on his face for hours now. She was breathing life back into him, and he didn't want it to ever end. She was like a drug, and he would always crave the way she made him feel.

He took a deep breath and let the fresh air fill his lungs. His mind was packed with thoughts of Addie, but having her here in his home was spinning his train of thought in a different direction.

He looked out into the open moonlit pasture of rolling hills behind the house and wondered again what he was going to do with this place. He had been pushing this thought from his mind since he came home, but Addie's presence brought the future to the forefront of his mind.

He liked having her here in his family's home on the land where he had grown up. The thought of a woman with him in this place had never crossed his mind as an option when he had briefly thought about his plans in the past.

He was shocked out of his reverie when he heard the door squeak open and turned to see Addie standing hesitantly in the doorway. Her hair hung loose over her shoulders, and she was a vision of innocence. His blood boiled as his hate for Jason surged. How could Jason even think of hurting her?

"Everything all right?" he said with a calmness he didn't feel.

"Everything's fine. Am I interrupting?"

"Not at all. I'm just mulling over a few things. Care to join me?" She was nervous, and he hated that she wasn't always comfortable with him. Didn't she know he would never hurt her?

There would be no more thinking tonight. He'd watched her enough tonight that he couldn't bring himself to care about the house, the land, or anything except the fact that he was lucky enough to be back in her presence.

She was an open book, and her face kept no secrets. Her eyes gave her away every time. He remembered the fear seared on her face the night of the attack, the night they had met. Their meeting was bittersweet, but he was certainly thankful for the events that had led them to this point.

He wouldn't stop wanting to be with her. He could feel it. She had made a mark in his life, and sometimes you just knew when people were meant to stay a part of your world. He wanted her in his world. Maybe the world his life revolved around.

She reclined in the chair beside him and sucked in a deep breath of awe. "Look at the stars." Her voice was full of wonder. "I've never seen them so bright."

"We have an uninhibited view of the night sky around here. It makes you feel small, doesn't it?"

Her lips were parted slightly as she scanned the expanse of unattainable midnight wonders. "I've never seen anything so beautiful."

He stared at her, lost in the realization that these same stars had watched over her every night and drank in her wild beauty. "Me either." She really was the most beautiful thing he had ever seen.

They stayed quiet for a few minutes, but the silence didn't feel strained. It felt comforting. He wasn't the best at communicating, and he could sense when someone just needed to be around another person.

When she finally spoke, she didn't raise her eyes to him and merely looked at her hands as if she could see the words she wanted to say written on her skin.

"I wanted to save myself. I wanted to be strong enough to save myself. I've felt weak and helpless my whole life." Her voice was choked and thick.

He called himself to the acknowledgement of what she meant, and he understood. The wild night sky could draw secrets out of a stone. She was giving him a part of her struggle. He had been so wrapped up in his need to protect her that he had taken the part of her independence he had meant for her to keep. He stood and closed the small space between them in no time, pulling her from her seat and wrapping her in his arms and resting his cheek against her silken hair.

She smelled slightly of coconut and vanilla as he whispered into her ear, "I'm sorry. Not for hurting him or saving you, but for taking that victory away from you." She clung to him, digging her claws into his shoulders. "The person you've become since you left him is your victory. You saved yourself when you were strong enough to leave and make a life of your own. Now it's time to protect the life you want. I'm going to be right here doing whatever it takes to make you happy." He fiercely placed his hands on both sides of her face as he pulled back to look at her. "I see your fire. I can teach you self-defense. You'll get stronger, and you won't have any reason to be afraid of him anymore."

Her appreciation was written on her face. "I would love that."

He should have thought of it sooner. It would make him feel better, too, knowing she could protect herself when they were apart.

She gave him a knowing look and ventured a small smile. "Tell me something about yourself, Declan. I don't know you, but…" She trailed off, and a spark of hope lit in his chest.

"But what?"

"I want to know you. I know it's hard for you to open up, so I understand if you don't want to talk. I just... want to understand why. I've had a difficult time knowing who to trust since I came here, but you've been easy."

He let his hands fall from her face, but she followed them down and cradled them in hers. Her hands were so small compared to his working hands. His hands had built homes, dug ditches, fixed cars…

His hands had killed.

Her hands were practically untouched, and as much as he wanted them to stay that way, he knew she wanted something different. This woman had confided to him that she was completely invested in finding Jason when she confessed that she had wanted to save herself, and that admission had meant more than just her acceptance of him and his ability to protect her. It meant that she trusted him, and she would be working with him, beside him, in this dangerous game they were playing.

She had shared a lot of herself with him, and he owed her the same as she had given him. It was easy to see why she still felt so far away from him when he kept himself wrapped up.

He bent, cradled her in his arms, and sat in a lounge chair with her curled in his lap. She laid her head against his chest and tilted her head to the heavens, still in awe of it all.

He would slowly ease her into his story, but he wanted to tell her everything. He knew he was meant to share this with her.

"When you came outside, I was thinking about what I should do with this place. My mother's family has owned and farmed this land for over a hundred years. Every generation that showed interest inherited the property. It's mostly been used for cattle, hay, and chickens, but there have been gardens and pigs in the past.

"My mom's name was Suzie. She was an only child, and she knew one day this land would be hers. So when she married Jeff... sorry, my dad, my grandparents had no problem letting them build this house on the property."

Now for the tricky part. "My parents had me soon after they married, and everyone started noticing that my dad was a little... off. He wasn't the respectful, caring man he had made himself out to be in the beginning of his relationship with my mom. My grandparents lived so close, they picked up on the tension in my parents' relationship. You can see how word of an unhappy marriage would travel quickly on this hillside.

"My mom grew to dislike him, but she was too sweet to say it outright. My grandparents certainly didn't like him, but they cared too much about their daughter to say anything. My dad would leave periodically while I was growing up. Sometimes, he would be gone for a few days, but the longest was a year and a half while I was in high school. When he came home, I asked him why he came back. He just said he felt obligated to be here, but he said it like a curse."

"Is that why you stayed home sometimes?"

She was putting the pieces together on her own. "Yeah. I couldn't stand the idea that Mom would think I had left her too. I couldn't stand her being here alone."

She was rubbing her fingertips up and down his forearm now, and he knew she was steadying him for the part that would hurt. Talking came easier with touch. Sometimes, it's easier to feel what to say and absorb what is being said.

"My mom died of breast cancer when I was eighteen. They caught it late because no one expected it. She was so young and healthy, until suddenly she wasn't."

He couldn't think about her in those few weeks before she died. The awful decline of her light and life. It was the worst injustice. The murder of innocence.

"I was about to graduate high school, and she was my world. I was the man of the house, since we could never rely on my dad, and my life revolved around her. It seemed like my world changed in a split second because it happened so fast. Within a few weeks, I had no one to care for and love anymore. My grandparents loved me, sure, and my friends were always around, but I wasn't sure I could ever care for someone like I did her. She was good down to her bones, and she always put me first, even when I was trying to put her first. My dad never came back after she died."

Addie's fingers had halted and her shoulders shook with the effort of breathing evenly. He stroked her hair and pulled her a little closer.

"I'm sorry. I didn't mean to upset you. It's in the past, and everything is fine now. I joined the Army right out of high school, and I haven't been back for any amount of time to make note of since I left, except for when my grandparents died. I was allowed to be at each of their funerals. My dad signed the house over to my grandparents when my mom died. He didn't want to live here, and he didn't want to be responsible for the taxes and upkeep either. Part of me wonders if he felt like he owed them something for the way he treated their daughter.

"My grandparents left this place to me, and I've been trying to decide what to do with it. I've been living here since I came back because the idea of looking for another place to live just seems about as exciting as watching paint dry." She gave him a bubbly chuckle that told him she was relaxing now that the worst was over.

They sat in silence for a while and time flowed together. He stroked her hair and wondered what a life with Addie here on his family land could be like. Would she like that? Why was he even thinking about a life with her after knowing her such a short amount of time? It had been a week since they met and formed the fake relationship that still cast a cloud over their budding real relationship. Surely, it was just the fact that having a woman here was unexpected. It felt more like home with Addie around. He hadn't been looking for someone, and a relationship hadn't crossed his mind until now.

Maybe she would like this place. Maybe she would want to be here with him. Jason had taken so much from her, but he wanted to give her everything. These stars could be hers, overlooking her fields and trees. He would love to give this to her if it was what she wanted. He knew then that he wouldn't make any decisions about this place until he knew where Addie fit into his life.

He looked down to find her asleep, and he couldn't help but stare as the most peaceful creature folded in his arms constricted his chest and claimed him body and soul. He wanted her to be his, and he wanted to be hers. He wanted to share with her this feeling she had given him in their short time together. He held her a little longer and his chest tightened when he wondered how long it would be until he could hold her like this again. They both had reasons for guarding their hearts, but perhaps this was the beginning of change.

He tilted his head to the sky and said a silent prayer. *God, if it's Your will, I'd ask for Addie to stay. I pray You'll show me how to be a better man so I can be a good companion for her. Show me the way, Father.*

Her phone buzzed in her pocket, and she woke up slowly. She gave a small stretch in his arms before realizing where she was. "Oh no, I fell asleep. I'm sorry." Her phone was a blinding light in the darkness surrounding them. The screen read Karen Jackson below the time near one in the morning.

"You better answer that. She's probably worried." He stretched his legs but kept his arms around her as she told Karen she fell asleep and would be home in about fifteen minutes.

Declan listened to her talking with her aunt and wondered how this woman had tied him up so tight. The worst part was that he really didn't care. He was happy to be captivated by her.

Chapter Fourteen

Adeline

Addie's Friday work shift seemed infinite. She and Declan had plans to go out for dinner, and her excitement was overshadowing the mundane duties of the day. Finally, closing time rolled around, and she waved good-bye to Libby and Amy as she met Declan at the door before he could take a full step inside the salon.

"You ready?" he asked with a smile on his face that said he already knew the answer.

"I've been waiting very impatiently all day for you to pick me up. I'm more than ready." She settled into the passenger's seat of his truck and leaned over to plant a quick kiss on his lips before buckling her seatbelt.

"Have you decided where you want to go for dinner tonight?" Declan asked as they drove toward Karen and Butch's house. "Is it still all right if the guys meet us there?"

"Sure. I've really wanted to try out Rusty's. Brian told me he plays there on the weekends sometimes." She hadn't been to most of the places in town, so she was happy to be going anywhere.

"Rusty's is great. I know the guys like it, and I think you will too. The food is pretty good for a biker restaurant."

"That sounds perfect."

Hopefully, this would be a fun night. With the lingering fact that Jason still wanted to kill her shoved into the back of her mind, she decided to trust Declan and his friends for a carefree night of fun. No one had heard a word about Jason since he attacked her in the alley, and she couldn't help thinking that no news was good news. Maybe he had decided to go home and forget about her. If she could only be so lucky.

"I'll let the guys know."

They pulled into the driveway, and Addie opened the truck door before Declan had come to a complete stop. She was more than ready to get her date with Declan started, even if their friends were joining them. "Great. Come inside. I'll be ready in twenty minutes."

She made her greetings to her aunt and uncle before rushing off to get ready. She quickly washed up and changed into a comfortable sundress to match her light-hearted mood.

She was gathering her makeup and cleaning off the vanity when she looked up to catch sight of Declan watching her in the mirror. He stood behind her with both of his hands propped on the doorframe above his head. It seemed most of her paranoia about Jason had worn off, since she hadn't sensed him behind her. Declan was hard to miss.

He didn't say anything as he let his arms fall to his sides and bridged the small gap between them. She continued the silence as she turned to face him. She stood patiently waiting to see what he would do and find out why he had sought her out.

He studied her face without speaking for precious seconds that hung in the small room around them, and she took the time to drink him in. His thick, dark hair was still slightly damp from his post-work shower and his beard was neatly trimmed per Libby's orders. But if eyes were the windows to the soul, his were crystal clear.

When he finally moved, his lips landed soft and sure against hers. His mouth had known the way of hers from the first moment they touched, and she felt a tinge of happiness at the easy recognition she felt in him. He anticipated her next move and met her match for match.

He pulled away with a mischievous smile. "You're on the clock, missy. Your twenty minutes are running out."

"You're gonna be so impressed when I meet you at the door in three minutes."

He gave a noncommittal "Uh huh" as he took in her outfit.

She had chosen a white dress with cap sleeves that hugged her waist and gently fanned out around her knees.

"Do you like it?" She emphasized the word *you* to let him know that it mattered to her what he thought, not anyone else.

"Sweetheart, I like you in anything. You could wear a burlap sack and all the men would still be jealous that you're on a date with me." She rewarded him with a sweet kiss on the cheek. "Thank you. Thank you for everything."

When she left Louisiana, she had hidden herself away, but Declan had found her despite her best efforts. He had pulled her from the shadows and refused to be ignored. "I never let myself hope I would be able to go out and have fun like this when I first came here, especially not so soon."

He took her hands in his before answering. "The only thing I want you to do is enjoy yourself."

She couldn't stop smiling, and she was starting to feel like her face was broken.

He backed away from her without letting his gaze fall from hers. "Come on. There's something I want you to see."

"I'll be there in a minute."

A tickle ran down her spine as he left her to finish getting ready. She turned back to the mirror and saw the wonder in her reflection. She knew why he had come for her, and the realization formed a smile on her blushing face.

She finished getting ready, grabbed her purse, said a quick good-bye to her aunt and uncle, and stepped outside onto the front porch to join Declan. She smiled when she caught sight of him, and he pointed into the field to the right of the house.

"Look."

It was twilight, and the field was covered in fireflies as far as she could see over the gently rolling hills. She was speechless for a long moment as she took in their twinkling dance.

When she reluctantly broke the spell by turning to him, he was propped against the house with his arms crossed over his chest, staring at her like a statue. How long had she been standing there caught in a trance by the gift that nature had given them tonight? How long had he been staring at her?

"It's beautiful," was all her mind could think of to describe the network of lights before them.

"I know. God creates amazing things." He pushed off the side of the house and slowly made his way toward her without breaking eye contact. He could have blended into the night in his black T-shirt and dark hair.

What a story of contrasts they were, she in her white dress and he in his black shirt, coming together to dilute the world with gray. "I've never seen anything so beautiful in all my life." He cupped her face and placed a gentle kiss on her forehead.

Was he talking about the fireflies or her? Hope bloomed in her chest at the sentiment.

He grabbed her hand and led her from the porch to the truck. After he helped her into the truck on the passenger's side, he made his way around it and hopped in.

"Do you call them fireflies or lightning bugs?" she asked casually, but her reason for asking felt anything but casual.

"Lightning bugs. Why? What do you call them?"

"I don't really know. My mom and dad always disagreed over the name. Every time we would see them, it would turn into a playful fight over what to call them, and they would each try to recruit me to their side. I could never choose a side. Now that they're gone, I still don't know what to call them."

She hadn't talked about her parents, other than to tell him they died when she was a teenager, but something about the appearance of the fireflies made her want to remember them and share something with him. Perhaps she felt turnabout was fair play, since he shared with her his family history under the stars.

"I think they would just be happy knowing you're still thinking about them when you see something so beautiful." He grabbed her hand and kissed it before setting their linked hands on her thigh. Touch with Declan had become important lately, and the recognition of positive touch kindled a feeling in her chest that gave her the courage to continue.

"My parents died from a car wreck when I was eighteen. My mom was killed on impact, but my dad lived about a day after the wreck." She wasn't sure if he wanted to hear this, but she knew it was important to share with him, since it explained a part of her past that was important to their mission to find Jason.

"I had been dating Jason for about six months at the time. We were in high school and had a carefree relationship that comes with no responsibility and a complete disregard for the future. We never talked about our future together. Before my dad died, we were in his hospital room, and I heard my dad ask Jason to take care of me. The doctors hadn't held out a lot of hope for his survival. I was young and scared out of my mind at the thought of losing my parents when I still needed them so much."

She still needed them now. Some days, she felt like she needed them more than anything. It was easy to feel alone when your parents were gone.

"I was overwhelmed with grief at the time, but later when I thought back on that moment, I remembered that Jason never answered my dad. He just looked from my dad to me and said 'She'll be fine' before he left the room. I never brought that up, but Jason used my dad's request against me throughout our relationship. He would basically complain that a helpless young girl had been left in his care and there wasn't anything he could do about it. I could have come to live with Butch and Karen back then, but I wanted to finish high school in New Orleans with my friends. It wasn't long until I didn't have any friends left. At that time, Jason hadn't come to resent me yet. By the time things went south between us, I was trapped."

"Why did it take you so long to leave?" It wasn't an accusation, but a genuine concern.

"My parents had left a trust account to me, and it was enough to live on until I got out of school. It was even enough to go to college for a while. After they died, I was immobilized by grief. I couldn't get out of bed most days. I just laid around and cried all day. Jason convinced me that he would be better suited to manage my money for me, so I put his name on the account not long after my parents died. At the time, he seemed to be looking out for my best interests. About a year later, things had gotten rocky between us, and I wanted to leave him. When I went to the bank to withdraw some money, I found out he had drained the account."

"You're kidding." She could see his knuckles turning white as he gripped and wrung the steering wheel in fury.

"When I confronted him about it, he was furious that I didn't trust him. He told me he would manage my money, and he gave me a sort of allowance that was enough to buy groceries and things we needed around the apartment. He never allowed anything extra or frivolous. I wasn't allowed to go to college. He said it was because he didn't trust me. I never knew if he meant that he didn't trust me to stay faithful or he didn't trust me not to leave him. I'm sure I would have found out sooner that he wasn't really the marketing director he told me he was the entire time we were together. He wouldn't let me have a job, and he always reminded me that I was lucky to be able to stay at home because he was providing for me. I could have made my own way in life if he hadn't stolen my money. After that, he dictated everything about my life. I couldn't see a way to leave him with no money."

She was quiet for a moment while she tried to relax and remove the lump from her throat. She couldn't look away from the road in front of her. Her vision was restricted to what the headlights allowed her to see.

"Sometimes, when I think of moments in my past, I have to ask myself if it was real or something I've dreamed, especially about my parents. Some parts of my life feel like stories I've heard or read a long time ago. Some of the stories I love, and I play them over and over again and wish I could reach out and touch them again, just have that happiness again. I try to convince myself I can slip back into that time, that place, that feeling, but it's never the same the second time around. It's dulled."

She swallowed hard and picked at her fingernails. "Other memories come to me in paralyzing flashes. I see the past for the span of a heartbeat as clear as day, just sitting on a bed as I enter a room, and it takes all of my control to keep going as if nothing had happened. Because it didn't. Not really. Sometimes, I feel a cold hand grip my neck in the stillness of the night like he might have if I had stayed longer. Sometimes, I feel the tackling impact of an airbag smash my chest in an instant while driving down a road I've never known. And for that split second, I almost believe I can feel the pain all over again. That pain I never really knew. The pain that killed my parents."

He didn't interrupt. He continued to let her open up to him. "Every time I'm caught unawares by my past, I wonder if it was real or part of a dream that has been sitting hidden in the back of my mind waiting to scare me… or remind me."

She hung her head, and a single teardrop fell into her lap without touching her cheek. "I feel like I failed my parents. They gave me a good life and set me up for a decent future. They taught me to be strong and independent, but I let Jason break me slowly over time. Look what I've done with my life." She threw her hands in the air in an all-encompassing gesture.

"I'm twenty-four years old, and I'm starting from the bottom. I ran away from what I thought was rock bottom to meet the real world like a slap in the face. Maybe that confidence my parents gave me was all fake. Maybe they saw more potential in me than what I actually have because they blindly loved me. The world is different and doesn't care about you or owe you any favors."

Her voice was higher and strained as she continued. "I miss them terribly, but my life with them feels like a dream instead of a memory. Sometimes, I wonder if I made up that happy life with them. Jason never let me talk about them, and sometimes the need to talk about them clawed at my insides, screaming to get out. He always told me to 'Move on and quit being so depressing,' but I was drowning in my grief." She couldn't look at him sitting so close to her in the driver's seat right now.

"I let Jason push me away from God. He didn't let me go to church. He didn't let me talk about God or anything close to my faith. I was trapped, and I just accepted it. I didn't fight back. Now that I'm free, I've been too scared to go back to church. I'm scared I've messed up too much with God."

Her chest hurt, and the real pain of all she had lost swirled in front of her. Declan squeezed her hand in comfort, and that was all she needed. He was letting her spill her soul without interrupting, and she squeezed his hand back. They rode in silence for a while, but silence never felt empty with him. He held her hand like a lifeline, and she knew he was still there with her. Not only physically, but he was mentally present with her in her moment of recollection.

He spoke suddenly and unexpectedly, killing their silence. "Jason couldn't take you away from God because God never left you. I can say that with all confidence. You can go back any time."

He rubbed his thumb over the back of her hand. "You are strong and independent. I see it in you. I have no obligation to fill your head with false hope like you think your parents may have done. I'm an unbiased bystander, and I can honestly say I feel deep down in my bones that you could do most anything you set your mind to. You have a drive in you that I can't help but admire. I've been coasting around here, getting lulled into the slow-paced life, and I see now that I've missed that motivation in myself. I haven't pushed myself into anything but my business with Dakota since I left the Army. I've watched you take control of your life lately, and I'm ashamed of myself for becoming so complacent. You've lit a fire in me in a short amount of time."

He started to fidget in his seat as he drove, and she knew he was well outside his comfort zone talking to her about this. "I have a confession to make myself. I've only been to church once since I came home from the Army. I made it through the service, but I felt like I was suffocating by the time I got in my truck after. There were just…"

When he didn't go on, she finished the thought for him. "Too many people?"

"Yes. I kept myself away from God because I couldn't stay calm around all those people."

It always amazed her how well Declan understood her. Would she ever be able to thank him for helping her heal? When she shared her deepest flaws, he opened up to her and showed her, instead of telling her that they were the same.

A thought came to her that brought instant calm. "Do you think we could help each other?"

"I like to think you're helping me every day."

"No, I mean maybe we should go to church... together." The idea that he could reject her had her chest tightening in an instant. This request seemed too important to be turned down. She needed him, and he needed her, but they both needed to get closer to God.

"I think that's a great idea. Butch and Karen go to the same church I grew up in. You want to start there?" He paused to glance at her as he drove and found her nodding wildly. Words failed her. "You're a terrifying wildfire drawing me out of a deep sleep. You have powers you haven't even begun to harness, and I think there is a good chance that you're the key to helping me get myself right with God too."

She stared at him as she absorbed his acceptance and confession. Her? Powerful? She felt so small and insignificant. She was honored that he would take that chance with her. They had looked at the stars together and felt smaller than a drop in the ocean, and he was telling her she was important.

She wasn't terrifying. He was.

Declan was not only making her have faith in herself, but supporting her and agreeing to work beside her to change the fate she had been merely accepting before he showed her that she could have more. She could have her relationship with God back. She realized that while she had been fighting for the future she wanted, God had been fighting for her, beside her, every step of the way.

She knew that she wanted a future that included this fearless man, and she could only hope he continued to want the same. He could run at any time, and she certainly didn't want another man feeling like she was his responsibility. She was no man's obligation, but she knew it was going to gut her if he decided her baggage was too much to bear. But with God between them, she felt their bond was stronger.

Staring out the window as they drove to meet his friends for dinner, she was brought to the surface of her drowning thoughts when he gently squeezed her hand. She looked down at the hand that sat on her thigh and had been held by his the entire ride and couldn't help the small smile she gave. He hadn't left her for a second as she revealed her less-than-desirable past to him. She felt a pang of shame and wanted to kick herself for doubting this selfless man who hadn't once mentioned leaving her to deal with her problems on her own.

She was a stranger to trust, but Declan had come into her life guns blazing and was blasting through her fortress one wall at a time.

Chapter Fifteen

Declan

Rusty's parking lot was starting to fill up, and Declan was forced to park behind the building.

"Wait here." He jumped out and ran around the front of the parked truck to open her door.

"Well, aren't you a true Southern gentleman." She may have been picking at him, but her genuine smile and sparkling eyes said she really was impressed by the gesture.

They entered the restaurant to find every table full. A small, slightly elevated stage was nestled in the far right corner of the room across from the bar. He had spent many nights here with his friends before they were old enough to drink. He hadn't been to Rusty's many times since he had been home, but somehow it looked exactly the same as it had eight years ago.

He spotted his friends at a table in the back near the bar and grasped Addie's hand in his. He led her to the table and pulled out an empty seat for her.

She gave a small wave and said, "Hey, guys." Each of his friends greeted her, and she ordered a sweet tea while he requested water.

Jake was still wearing his deputy uniform, Brian was setting up his equipment at the makeshift stage in the corner of the room, and Dakota sat with his arms crossed in front of a glass of water as he listened to Marcus describe his latest car project.

He watched Addie as the men settled into a comfortable banter. She even began to relax herself, until Ian made his appearance at the table with his perpetual bad attitude. When Ian launched into a rant about work, the guys sighed and tried to steer him toward a safe topic. Next, Dakota mentioned singing karaoke, and the others gave booming laughs before Brian told him to "leave it to the gifted."

He couldn't take his eyes off Addie throughout the night, but he caught her watching him too. He was probably making her uncomfortable, because her cheeks were pink as she watched him over her glass.

He leaned over to whisper in her ear once their meal was finished and the waitress took their plates. "Every man in this place is wishing you were here with him."

Without looking around the room to see if he was right, she turned to him. He was leaning toward her with his weight resting across the back of her chair, his lips a mere inch from touching hers, and his gaze was locked on her mouth. She proudly lifted her face to his and said with a knowing smile, "I'm glad I'm here with you."

He didn't hesitate, but he slowly closed the distance between them and wrapped his arm around her shoulder pulling her closer and into a quick, deep kiss. She tasted like sweet tea and barbecue sauce, and he knew he would chase that combination for the rest of his days. When they finally disengaged, his body tingled like the buzz from a shot of something harder than water.

"I love your laugh. It's beautiful, and I want to keep you smiling and laughing all the time." He leaned in, gently brushing his lips to her ear.

Her smile grew wider, and he realized how corny his confession sounded, but for once he couldn't bring himself to care. He was being honest, and right now he didn't feel his normal urge to stay reserved and quiet. He didn't express his feelings or even his thoughts much, but when he did, he simply said what he meant.

When they came back to the present, he noticed all of his friends had made their way closer to the stage where Brian carefully placed a microphone before him. When Brian greeted the crowd, every patron shouted or whistled in anticipation of the show. His friend didn't make the fans wait as he promptly began playing a well-known country song that had everyone rising to their feet.

"You want to dance?" she asked, and he could tell she hadn't put a lot of effort into the request, knowing his tendency to hang around the walls instead of the dance floors.

"Sure. Let's go." They made their way to the open floor where everyone swayed to the beat.

The song was fast, and Addie jumped right into the fray like a ballerina beginning her paralyzed dance, as soon as the music box is wound tight. Seeing how animated she became reinforced her love of music.

She swayed with him from time to time, but he could tell his inability to dance was hindering her. Still, she never let the smile fall from her face.

After a few songs, she turned to him and whispered in his ear above the music, "Can we go home?"

At first, he hadn't understood her question. She was having fun, right? "We can stay if you want."

She shook her head to convey her meaning above the noise. "No, I'd rather spend time with you."

His chest tightened at her admission, but he grabbed her hand and led her toward their table where Marcus and Dakota sat talking. She grabbed her purse and they said quick good-byes to their friends. She waved over her head to Brian on stage as they made their way to the door.

When they had settled into the truck, he looked to her for direction. She had said "Can we go home," but did she mean drop her off at Butch and Karen's? She also said she wanted to spend time with him, and dropping her off at home sounded like an end to their date night.

"Where to, sweetheart?"

She took a deep breath and tapped her chin in a mock gesture of thinking. "Do you remember when I won our game where I guessed the songs on the radio?"

He smiled at the direction her thoughts were taking. She had a win to cash in. "I remember."

"Well, I think I would like to trade my winnings for a movie night at your house."

He laughed loud and merrily. "You don't have to spend your win on movie night. I'd do it without being forced. Save your win for something good, like asking me to shop with you or asking me to go to a Christmas party."

He noticed she hadn't laughed at his suggestion, and he turned to find her studying him. "Do you think I would want you to do things like that with me knowing they're difficult for you? I hate seeing you in those uncomfortable situations."

Addie never faltered in her care for others. He had seen it enough now to know it was genuine, and it warmed him from the inside out.

"I don't think that, but I would have to be really bad off not to be able to joke with you about my problem. Yes, some times are worse than others, but when you're around, it really isn't so bad. That's why doing those things with you wouldn't be as bad as they sound or as hard as they would have been before you."

"I'm glad, but I'm still not dragging you through a mall anytime soon."

When they arrived at the house, Declan relaxed on the couch with his legs stretched out straight and scratched Reaper's ears while he waited for Addie to choose a movie.

Addie settled on a rom-com, but he didn't mind in the slightest. He wouldn't be able to pay attention to the movie anyway. He was too busy watching her and taking her in. The smell of sugar and vanilla wafted around him as she settled on the couch beside him. He could be hypnotized by that smell.

"Have you seen this one before?" she asked as she sat beside him, pulling a blanket into her lap.

He was sure she already knew the answer, so he gave a rumbling chuckle. "No. Have you?"

"No. Before I moved in with Butch and Karen, I hadn't watched a movie since I was in high school, before… things changed."

His heart broke a little more for her. Something as simple as enjoying a movie had been taken from her.

"Jason came home one day about four years ago and found me watching a movie." She was watching the television screen now, but he knew she was replaying a scene from the past in her head. "He was furious. I was lazy. I was worthless. And if I had enough time to sit around watching television all day, then I must have too much free time on my hands. I wasn't proving to be a good investment."

Red tinged the edges of his vision as she spoke the last word like a curse. Was she serious? An investment?

"After that, he gave me more errands to run for him, but he made sure to keep me on a tighter leash. I had to report in to him more with updates and locations."

"I'm sorry you had to go through that." He pulled her attention away from the movie she hadn't really been seeing. Gripping her chin, he forced her to look at him as he spoke slowly and clearly. "It's over now. You don't have to be afraid of him anymore."

Her face didn't move, but her eyes were downcast. She couldn't let him see that she still didn't believe she was out of the woods Jason had trapped her in for so many years.

She gently tugged her chin from his grasp and adjusted her position on the couch with a sigh. She was letting him know that the conversation was over, and she adopted a practiced smile to hide her misgivings.

She moved a little closer to him so their knees were touching before she crossed her legs at the knee, letting her calf cross over his. They were too close, and he forced himself to keep his attention on the movie. He might not have been interested in the scene playing on the television, but he would make sure she enjoyed every second of this movie and any other she wanted to watch with him.

He could give her these small kindnesses, and he would hope they would make up for the things he couldn't give her. He had no illusions about being a perfect man, and for once his shortcomings terrified him. They had the power to cost him the happiness sitting curled into his side.

As the end credits played and Addie smiled up at him like she had just received her own happy ending, he couldn't stop himself. Without thinking twice, he slipped his arm over her shoulders and pulled her flush with his body. The way she fit against him felt perfect and right. Her small frame fit under his large wing like the missing piece of a puzzle, an anticipated completion that settled his raging blood. He instinctively leaned in and kissed the top of her head. She turned to face him, and he couldn't stop himself when his gaze locked on her full lips.

He should kiss her. He wanted her lips on his more than anything right now. Nothing was holding him back. Her lips were bare, and that was how he wanted it to stay. He didn't want even a slight barrier between them. He wanted to taste *her*, not some lip paint. Her eyes locked on his, and he hesitated only one moment to make sure this was what she wanted, but he only saw happiness. The same happiness he found when he was with her.

His mouth sealed with hers as he pulled her tighter to him, crushing her to his chest. Her lips were softer than anything he could have imagined, and he drank them in. They had shared small kisses throughout their days, but nothing like this. He had been dreaming about this for weeks. She had consumed his every thought since he first saw her. He was glad they had taken things slow because the reward was worth the wait.

When they broke the kiss, he knew he had to tell her how he felt about her. He didn't want her thinking he was only looking for one thing with her. He wouldn't allow it. No, he wanted the long run with her, and he wanted her to know how much she had come to mean to him. He wanted to be everything her last relationship wasn't. He wanted their connection to be better than either of them had ever experienced.

"I care about you, Addie. I need you to know that I want this to be real between us. It's not all about working at my grandparents' house or making sure Jason can't get to you. I really want to be with you."

She put her hands on his face and forced him to look at her. She forced him to look into her soft blue eyes and see her. She was calming him with her actions, her presence, before she even spoke.

"I want to be with you too, Declan. I don't know what the future holds, but I can see that this could be good for both of us. I see this as the beginning of a long adventure with you. I don't just see you as protection. I see you for who you are as a person. You're a man who has given himself wholeheartedly for a stranger. You've shown me so much of yourself, and I want more. I want all of you. I want to make you as happy as you've made me." She paused. "I want you to let me in too."

Her thumbs gently stroked his beard, calming him enough to realize what she was saying. "You're dangerous." He took one of her hands in his and studied it, inspecting every angle as he spoke. "You're the only woman who has ever made me feel anything. I'm afraid I'll be happy with you... then you'll realize there are better things out there. I'm afraid of what knowing how amazing you are will do to me when it's all gone."

"I'm scared too, but this doesn't have to be something with an expiration date. This is new for both of us. We can learn together."

He kissed her again. The heat from earlier was still fierce, but the impatience was gone. He had all the time in the world to savor her.

In that moment, a shot in the night, a combination of shattering glass and the boom of a firearm filled the room, and his years of living in anticipation in the Army kicked in. He rolled Addie onto the floor beneath his body just as the second shot rang through the house.

Another and another. He counted five shots moving from the living room where they lay surrounded by shards of glass toward the bedrooms on the western side of the house.

Just as fast as they had begun, the shots were over, but Addie's heavy breathing remained in his ear. Reaper bolted into the room barking in fear.

"What was that?" Her voice and her body shook as she lay trapped between his complete body weight and the sea of glass littering the carpet.

He pulled his cell phone from his pocket as he eyed the broken window wall facing the road. "I would bet good money that was Jason."

He dialed Jake and got a quick answer. "Hey, Dec—"

"Can you get someone to my house? I think Jason just did a drive by shooting on the house. Five shots. Sounded like an AR-15."

"I'm on it. You need paramedics?"

"No, just law enforcement."

He hung up the phone and handed it to Addie. "If Jake calls back, tell him I'm checking to see if anyone is outside, and try to stay on the phone with him as long as you can."

She grabbed at the phone with two shaky hands and held it like a lifeline. He hated seeing her scared, but this was his element. He hoped she trusted him.

Declan turned to Reaper and waved him over, "Stay here with Addie." The dog's cries ceased, and he laid his entire body on the floor beside her legs.

He cradled her face in his hands and focused on calming her. "Listen to me. You're all right. I think they just drove by, but I need to know for sure. Jake will be here soon. I'm going outside, but I'll hurry. Stay here until I get back. Don't move." He palmed the side of her face and stroked a thumb across her eyebrow as he spoke. She seemed slightly calmer by the time he had finished talking.

"Okay. Please be careful." She eyed the broken window like the devil himself might be waiting just outside. "If that was Jason, it was only a message."

He knew exactly what Jason was saying. *I see you.*

"I know. I got the message. Don't worry about it. I promise I'll be careful." He pushed himself from the floor and grabbed a gun he kept hidden on top of a bookshelf filled with more picture frames and figurines than books. He hadn't cared to get rid of the shelf after his mother died, and it served as a good hiding spot. He had at least one gun hidden in every room of his house.

He checked the pistol and tucked it in close to his body as he opened the front door and stepped out onto the porch. The night was quiet, and the new moon was useless. He quickly checked both ways, keeping a close eye on the front door as he slid along the wall to the corner of the house.

The eastern perimeter seemed clear, and he retraced his steps to check the western side. He knew the western side of the house facing the woods was the more likely hiding spot for someone who intended to check in on the house, but he saw no sign of anyone. Not even a whisper of a squirrel in the trees. Maybe nature hadn't returned to its normal rhythm yet, after the shock of the gunshots.

He didn't waste time with stealth as he headed back into the house and let Addie know to stay where she was while he checked the back. French doors lined the back wall of the kitchen and provided no place to hide from someone who wanted to peek in. There would be no discreet search on this side of the house.

By the time he was finished checking around the house, he could hear sirens in the distance. Jake must have already been on his way home to make it here so quickly. When Jake arrived, he and his friend made another check around the house before another deputy arrived, but still found nothing.

Jake made a beeline straight for Addie when they entered the house. She was sitting on the couch with Reaper's head in her lap clutching Declan's phone to her chest. "It had to be Jason, right? Or at least someone working with him. No one else has it out for you." Jake gently tilted her head back and forth, checking for injuries. Her bruises were healed now, but a few of the cuts from the first time Jason had attacked her were beginning to form pink scars. "Are you hurt?"

"No, I'm fine. Declan was so… fast. He got us both down before anything could even get to us." She recounted the tale as if Declan were a superhero who had swept in to save her in the shadows of the night.

"I'm glad y'all are both all right. You gotta stop calling me like this, Dec." Jake shook his head as if his friend had pulled a girl's hair on the playground.

"You gotta find some way to get this guy out of the picture. He can't keep harassing Addie like this. She can't even live her life for fear he's going to be around the next corner." Declan swept his arm out to indicate Addie's hunched posture. Jason was on his last nerve.

Jake winced. "I'm trying my best. We're short staffed, and there isn't even any money in the budget to hire right now. We're running on fumes and prayers, Dec. I'm trying."

Declan heaved a deep sigh and ran his fingers through his hair. "I know. I'm sorry. It's not your fault this guy is playing cat and mouse with her. I just need her safe."

"Trust me. I need her safe too. This guy is dangerous, and I can't seem to get ahead of him. He's slick. I'm sorry, Addie."

She stepped forward, still clutching the cell phone. "It's all right. I know you're trying. Thank you for getting here so quickly."

Jake turned to inspect the broken window wall. "You said you're staying with Butch and Karen?"

"That's right."

The other deputy stepped across the broken glass toward them. "Karen is going to lose her mind when she hears about this." Joe was an old buddy from high school. They had lost touch after graduation, but Declan would trust Joe to help Jake get the job done.

"Tell me about it. She might not let Addie come out and play with me anymore." Declan wrapped his arm around her shoulders, and she visibly relaxed at his joke.

"Joe and I are gonna finish up our investigation, then we can get you home, Addie. Dec, you wanna pack a bag and stay in the guestroom tonight? I'll help you fix this window tomorrow."

Declan pulled his arm from around Addie's shoulders and clapped his friend on the back. "Thanks, man. I appreciate that. I'll grab some stuff and meet you there with Reaper after I drop Addie off at her place."

Declan packed a quick bag and promised Addie a redo on their movie night. They didn't say much on the way to Butch and Karen's. Holding hands was enough comfort for both of them.

He knew without a shadow of a doubt he would protect her at any cost. He just wished he knew how to get her out of harm's way so she could breathe a little. When would her hiding stop? Where was this man's line? Would he keep making such drastic moves?

When he pulled into the drive at Butch and Karen's house, a more immediate fear hit him in the face. How was he going to explain this to them? They trusted him to protect her, and they had come so close to losing tonight.

He turned to her and gave her hand a squeeze. "Let's do this."

Addie seemed reluctant to have the talk, too, as she slowly slid from the passenger's side. He met her at the front of the truck and wrapped his arm around her. "I'm here now, and Jake promised me he would have a patrol nearby all night. He can't get to you, as long as we're prepared."

"I know, but I hate the way he keeps interrupting your life. I brought this problem to town, and it seems like everyone else is suffering. I'll pay for your new window…"

He stopped her on the sidewalk and turned her to face him. "Listen, Addie. I don't regret one minute of time we've spent together. Just because we're weathering bad times doesn't mean I would ever wish to be anywhere else. You're what I care about."

The reality of his words was stark in the moonless night, and he prayed she took every word to heart.

"I wouldn't want to be anywhere else either. I'm so thankful you're in my life."

He shouldn't fear telling Butch and Karen about what happened tonight. He had kept her safe, and that would always be his goal.

"I won't be any good at this," he said, praying against all odds that they could overcome the unknown that lay before them.

When he searched her eyes, he saw that she knew what he meant. A relationship. A connection. She also gave him a look that said she didn't believe him. Neither of them knew how to have a healthy relationship. Her relationship experience was full of regret and suppression, while his was non-existent.

"I won't either, but maybe we can learn together." She was always looking on the bright side, and relief washed over him.

"That's all I ask. Be patient with me, and I'll try to give you the best of myself. You deserve it. I love your drive to live, your fight to do more than just survive. You pushed the demons that chased you to the side and refused to give up. You're so much stronger than you give yourself credit for, and I want to be worthy of that fierce strength."

"I don't want just the best of you. I want all of you. The ups, the downs, the good times, and the hard times. It's not going to be roses all the time, but I think you and I can do it... together."

He couldn't imagine going through his life without her now. Of course, he wanted to face everything with her. She made him better, and he loved her for the amazing way she made him feel like he was worthy.

He loved her. He thought he loved her. Did he even know what love was?

He had spent many years guarding his heart from the world, being let down time and time again by a father who should have loved him, and mourning the loss of the one person who had loved him unconditionally. Now he was giving himself to Addie in mind, body, and soul, and he was terrified.

Of all the times he had missed his mother since she died, he missed her now the most. He wanted her opinion, her advice. He wanted to tell her about Adeline, the woman who had consumed him.

CHAPTER SIXTEEN

Adeline

Addie fumbled with the hem of her shirt and made a conscious effort not to bite her fingernails. She was still reeling from the shooting last night, and constantly looking over her shoulder was exhausting.

Jason made his presence known last night, and the echoes of violence still rang in her blood. That's what Jason wanted. He wanted her to feel him watching her. He wanted her to suffocate on her paranoia. It was working. She couldn't keep her mind on her job, and Amy and Libby had long since stopped trying to carry on casual conversation with her today.

She kept trying to push her thoughts to happier topics. She couldn't stop thinking about their conversation last night before the onslaught had shattered the semblance of peace and joy. She touched her lips gently, remembering the way he had kissed her, and for once she didn't have the urge to chew on the fingernails that hung suspended so close to her waiting teeth.

She knew it in her bones that this was where she belonged. Declan was meant to be part of her world, and she was meant to be part of his. Their lives had been intertwined from the moment he saved her.

She couldn't remember feeling so at ease around someone who wasn't her family, and she couldn't help but wonder if she was being naive. Maybe she was rushing things with him to fill a void of loneliness in her life. She didn't know how rebounds worked, but her connection with Declan didn't feel as insignificant as a rebound.

In all honesty, she hadn't been the least bit broken up about the demise of her relationship with Jason. What could she possibly be upset about? She didn't miss him or the life they had somewhat shared together. She was better off without him in every way, but the best part about their split was that she was free to be herself. For the first time in years, she could make her own decisions.

She tried to focus her attention on her work, but her motivation had taken the day off.

Today had been the first day it had rained in a week and a half. It was Saturday, so Declan had gotten up early to install the new windows with Brian and Jake before taking her out to breakfast before work. He had been working at his grandparents' house ever since.

He had been reluctant to spend so much of the day away from her, and she had agreed to help some more at his grandparents' house when she got off work. He promised to pick her up at the end of her shift.

They had found a productive system and were making better progress toward getting the house ready to rent out now. They had worked through two guest rooms, the dining room, and the bathroom. Declan was working in the basement today, since he had been putting it off. He took her downstairs to see it once, and her mouth had almost dropped in shock. The entire room was filled with stuff to the point that you couldn't create a path through the debris. She would bet her last week's paycheck you could find anything you were looking for in that unfinished basement if you had the time to sort through everything.

Declan showed up on time to pick her up from her shift and merely stood in the doorway to the salon. He was covered in dirt and dust from head to toe. His shirt had a white splash of what looked like paint beneath his left arm, and his beard was a slightly grayer shade of brown.

"What happened to you?"

Declan wasn't in a mood to pretend as he growled, "The basement happened. That place might be the death of me."

She wanted to laugh, but she knew he was serious. Apparently, his work day had been stressful. "I'm sorry. We don't have to go back this afternoon, if you're not up to it. You look like you've had enough."

"Nah. I'm fine. Sorry I didn't shower before coming. I just knew I was going to get dirty again and didn't see the point in it."

"No worries. I'll just grab my purse and we can head on over." After seeing how dirty Declan was, she was thankful she had worn something more practical to work today.

Declan's irritation seemed to have eased completely by the time they arrived at his grandparents' house. They grabbed more boxes and cleaning supplies from the back seat of the truck and jogged through the sprinkling rain to the door.

Entering the house now was a completely different experience. The living room was gaping and gutted without the menagerie of figurines that had adorned every surface on her first visit. The whole house had lost the remnants of life, other than the notches in the doorframe marking Declan's early growth. It no longer looked like someone had watched television or cooked breakfast on the stove only hours before. The house had been stripped of its memories.

Declan led the way deeper into the house and placed the items on the dining room table. "I actually started with the kitchen this morning and made it through that room. Most of the things in the kitchen are going to the church, so it was easy. The basement just turned into a disaster in a hurry. I hadn't been working down there long when I left to pick you up."

"Maybe it won't be so bad with two of us tackling it."

He shook his head. "Actually, I'd like to give the basement a rest today. I'm not ready to meet that old foe again. The paint got me before I even made it all the way down the stairs." He indicated the splash of white on his shirt.

"That's fine. We'll come back to it later when you've had some time to cool down." Addie patted his arm in understanding. "We're not in a hurry, remember?"

"Right. You want to start on the master bedroom? The alarm clock has a radio, and I'd like to listen to the Georgia game." He was asking her, but he didn't seem excited about the prospect of working on the master bedroom. It was the last room left to do upstairs, and she suddenly thought he might have been avoiding it as much as the basement, if not more.

"Sure. Let's go." She grabbed her cleaning supplies and followed him to the last bedroom on the left. The walls were dark wood paneling, and the bed was neatly made in a forest-green comforter with a handful of shams and throw pillows adorning the head.

He stopped just inside the room, and she didn't push him. "I don't even know where to start on this room." He adjusted the dial on the clock radio and sighed. "I guess I'll take the closet."

"I'll dust the fan and the headboards until you need me." They each took to their assignments, but she finished the higher dusting before he had even pulled all of the clothes from the closet or either football team had scored a touchdown. The closet was small, but dragging the clothes out was difficult in the tight space.

She went to grab some garbage bags from the dining room that housed their packing stash and returned to find the closet gutted of the remaining clothes and shoes.

She was quickly learning that his grandparents had taken meticulous care of the things they owned. The clothes, shoes, and necessities she saw were mostly outdated and worn, but completely usable. She also noticed they hadn't owned copious amounts of anything. There would be no excess found in this home, except the knickknacks, and she could imagine those comprised years of gifts.

Declan stood with his hands on his hips, staring at the clothes littering the bed. "I'm just going to pack these up for donation." His voice was as hollow as the closet, and she knew he was having a hard time stripping this home of the traces of the people he loved.

Addie didn't say anything. She just grabbed a rag and cleaner and began scrubbing the walls and doorframes of the empty closet. Once the tiny square of flooring was vacuumed, she wrestled the vacuum cleaner through the doorway and found Declan sitting on the floor with his back propped against the bed. Various books were spread out on the floor between him and an empty, half-opened dresser drawer.

He picked up the books one by one and placed them in a box on his left. Some he looked at more than others, but she could see now that most of them were devotionals. At the bottom of the pile was a book that was considerably larger than the others. Its mahogany cover caught her eye, and she could see it was probably a Bible.

She sat on the bed behind him and waited. She was curious about the Bible, but she didn't want to ask him if she could see it outright. She watched him stack the rest of the books into the box and stand to move it out of their way. He would take it to the kitchen to be taped up, labeled, and loaded into the truck.

As soon as he left the room, she got up from the bed, sat on the floor, and ran her fingers along the worn edge of the Bible. The name Margaret Jane Townley had been engraved in the bottom right of the front cover. The coloring had worn out of the embossing, but she could still make out the name. Townley must have been his grandmother's maiden name, judging by the age of the book.

She flipped open the first few pages to find faded gray ink running along neat lines. The entire page was filled with names and dates.

Births, deaths, and weddings. The next few pages were the same. Names and dates. But as she sat flipping the thin, transparent pages, she couldn't stop staring. These were family, friends, people who made Declan's grandmother's life brighter.

The last name on the list was written in the newest and darkest ink, but even this recording was slightly faded. Suzanne Janet Cooper King was printed in shaky handwriting. Her date of death was logged beside her name and birth date, just as all the others listed, but Addie's fingers shook as she traced the letters. The record of a life summed up in such few letters. She could see how the chronicle would have broken a mother's heart.

She heard Declan returning a moment too late but shut the Bible quickly on instinct. "I'm sorry." The apology was uttered within a second, but her heart pounded long after. She didn't want him upset seeing his mother's name chronicled alongside the day she died.

"For what?" he asked, genuinely puzzled.

She looked at the Bible sitting like a weight between them. "I was just looking, and I saw…" She swallowed the last word.

He crouched in the floor and opened the Bible. "Oh." She knew he realized what he would find if he flipped to the end of the list.

"Are you…are you going to keep it?" She had to know. When her own parents died, she hadn't been able to keep anything important. How she wished she had something from her own long-gone family to keep their memory alive. Being the only living person left in your family was a hard pill to swallow, and she and Declan were both close enough that it hurt.

He turned to her for a moment before bringing his attention back to the family Bible. "Yeah. Granny carried this Bible for years. My whole life. If it was stuck in a drawer, I doubt she carried it anymore after Mom died. She probably got a new one."

Addie could understand the sentiment. The Bible probably weighed more when your child's death was written in it.

She cupped her hands around her mouth in shock. God's son had died for her sins, and almost half of the book was a testament to His life and death. The Bible Declan held in his hands held the birth and the death of the Savior. The most important life and death the world would ever experience.

"Can I see it?" she whispered. She hadn't read a word from the Bible in years, and her eyes were starving for the words. She couldn't remember any of them, and her body felt empty of anything that mattered. All she could think about was how much of that book she could consume.

He handed it to her easily, and asked, "Do you have a Bible?"

She shook her head. "I haven't owned one in a while."

He tilted his head toward the book. "Why don't you keep this one for a while? You'll need one for church tomorrow, remember?"

He was right. They had decided to go to church together tomorrow. "Are you sure?" As much as this Bible meant to her, she knew it meant more to him.

"The Bible is the Bible. Sure there are different versions, and people usually have a preference, but I can read the same message in any Bible. The only difference is this one has a family tree in it. That list isn't as powerful as the words God gave us."

He was right. The most important part of this Bible or any Bible was the Word of God. Giving her access to what God wanted her to know meant more than his family legacy.

"Thank you." She hugged the Bible to her chest and her lower lip quivered. He didn't understand what he had given her. He was giving her the life she had always hoped to live. A life of love *and* freedom she had hardly dared to dream before. This was the happiness she had longed for all her life. Someone to stand by her in her life and her spiritual journey to become closer to God.

That small 'thank you' didn't seem to be enough. He had awoken her in so many ways. He pushed her to be strong and fight for herself, he never lost patience with her, he never complained about the situation she had brought to his door. He had fostered her weak heart and encouraged her to trust again. He showed her how to live again.

"I think we've done enough for tonight. Let's go get some pizza and I'll take you home."

As appealing as pizza sounded, she was more excited to get home and read. She was looking forward to tomorrow, and she hoped the day was easier for Declan than his last visit to church.

She knew the stakes of her freedom from Jason were higher than she realized. She was fighting for her relationship with God and her relationship with the selfless man who stood beside her. Now that she had set her mind to preserving the things that mattered most, losing wasn't an option.

CHAPTER SEVENTEEN

Adeline

Addie arrived at Declan's house for breakfast around seven the next morning. The door was open, so she let herself in to find him in the kitchen already cooking breakfast. He knew which foods were her favorites now, but she noticed that he tried to mix in something different as often as he could just to see if he could find new things she liked.

She tiptoed into the kitchen with the biggest smile on her face. As if she couldn't contain the happiness inside of her, she blurted, "Good morning, handsome," followed by a determined kiss.

"Morning, sweetheart. I wanted to get this started, but could you take over for a minute while I shower?"

"Absolutely." She took the pan from his hand before he kissed her head and went to shower. She began humming an old hymn she remembered from childhood, but soon she was singing the chorus. That song led into the next praise song she remembered, and the next, and the next.

She was knee deep in "Just as I am" when she turned to find Declan leaning against the doorframe with his arms crossed over his chest. He was silent and still, and she could imagine he had learned those traits from the Army.

The words of the song she had been singing echoed in her head. Declan had accepted her for who she really was, baggage, past, and all. Her Heavenly Father promised to do the same, and the recognition of acceptance made her heart soar.

He tilted his chin up and smiled. "You're gorgeous."

She looked down at the dress she had chosen for church this morning. It was a flowing sundress covered in pinks, oranges, and yellows that looked like a southern sunset. The dress had reflected her bright mood, happy and radiant enough to sing praises on a Sunday morning.

"Thank you. You're pretty handsome yourself." He was more than handsome, but there was no way to tell him so. He was selfless and kind in ways that made her thankful for knowing him because he made her want to be a better person. "How long have you been there?" She tucked her hair behind her ear and returned her attention to breakfast.

"Not long. You looked so happy, I didn't want to interrupt you. Plus, I thoroughly enjoyed the show."

He closed the small gap that separated them and gently touched his forehead to hers. "You have a beautiful voice."

She tilted her head up, and her cheeks were slightly pink from his compliments.

"Thank you." She gently touched her lips to his. "Breakfast is almost ready."

"Great. I'm starving." He squeezed her arms and gave her a wink before helping finish up breakfast.

The church was beginning to fill up when they arrived, and she spotted Brian closer to the altar talking to Marcus. A few preteens skipped around Marcus, and his eyes followed them while Brian rattled on. Declan warned her about Marcus' siblings. Apparently, he was their caretaker, and he took his responsibility seriously. Dakota sat on the second to last pew with a group of people who looked to be his family.

She stayed close to Declan as people began stopping him to talk, usually mentioning his absence or his time in the Army. Some even made comments about his choice of facial hair. A few people offered condolences on his grandparents' deaths. However, he seemed much more at ease than some of the other times she had seen him bombarded with questions or well wishes.

Declan began introducing Addie as his girlfriend with an enormous amount of pride. She greeted each person with a smile, happy to be by his side. A sharp pang hit her chest. Jason had tried to take this from her, and he had almost succeeded. She shuddered at the thought.

She hugged Butch and Karen when they arrived, and Declan followed her to shake hands with her family.

"Good morning, Karen. Butch," Declan said as they met.

"Good to see you, Dec, and good to know Addie is still all right. I can't say we haven't been more skittish after what happened the other night." Her Uncle Butch had been tough as nails her whole life, but he had a real soft spot for her.

"I'm glad she's all right too. Don't worry, Butch. She's safe with me." Butch had asked Declan to keep her safe, but he hadn't expected him to keep her happy too. He had done that on his own.

They took their seats next to Butch and Karen and settled in for the service. Addie got another chance to sing during the song service, and once again she felt the music in her bones. If God had asked her to make a joyful noise, she was sure this was what He meant. The power of the message resonated with her in a way she hadn't known she was missing all those years.

With Declan's family Bible in tow, she absorbed every word of the service. As the preacher spoke, her lungs constricted at the evidence she had been denying. She had once proudly served the Mighty God that filled these walls and this Bible before she had spent years dampening His presence in her life. How could she have ever doubted He would deliver her from her struggles? Nothing was beyond His capability.

Again, she was reminded that only God had the power to truly save her. The whole time she had been trying to save herself was a waste.

What really needed saving was her soul, but He was always with her. He never left her alone, even in her loneliest days. She could feel Him with her now.

Declan held her hand through the service. He seemed to be handling the experience well, while she was reduced to a red, teary face by the end of the service.

When the congregation was dismissed, fellowship commenced, and they met up with Marcus in the parking lot. Declan had breezed through the service without his normal sweaty hands and fidgeting, but she noticed the moment his fight or flight instincts kicked in when an older woman made eye contact with him across the parking lot and made her way toward them.

She watched his fight instinct win over by a small margin as the woman stopped in front of him with a look on her face that was anything but friendly.

"Well, well, well. If it isn't the ghost of a boy that ran away from home years ago. Declan King, is that you?" She grabbed his upper arm and gave a slight squeeze.

"Yes, Mrs. Miller. I've been back in Carson for a few months now." He crossed his arms over his chest in a closed-off stance that meant he wasn't up for her taunting.

"Oh, really? I haven't seen you out and about. I don't blame you. I would be scared to show my face around here too if I had abandoned my poor old grandparents on their deathbeds the way you did."

This woman was outright hateful, and Addie didn't have any use for that kind of attitude. Especially when the woman's hatred was directed at Declan.

Mrs. Miller gave a click of her tongue behind her teeth, and Addie could practically see his blood boiling as his jaw clenched.

Just as Declan opened his mouth to respond to her hateful comment, Addie stepped in front of him.

"Hi, I'm Adeline, Declan's girlfriend. I would say it's nice to meet you, but you just outright insulted my boyfriend, and first impressions mean a lot." She kept the smile on her face steady as she raised her eyebrows at the old coot daring her to retaliate.

Mrs. Miller's face turned red and her lips pursed into a line so thin they ceased to exist. She huffed a breath and glared at Declan. "You know, your father would want to know you're back in town." She walked away with her last jab hanging in the air.

Declan was tense and speechless. Addie knew he didn't need her to fight his battles for him, but she needed to say something to let that woman know it wasn't acceptable to talk like that to people.

Marcus was the first to speak. "Well, that was impressive."

Was that a comment of approval from Marcus? Things were definitely changing.

"She needs a swift kick in the butt for saying something like that to you. How dare she say such horrible things for no good reason." Addie was fired up, and her good mood from only moments ago was fading away.

"Marcus is right. That was impressive, but you need to forget about her. She's full of hate, and it spreads easily."

"You're right. I'm sorry. I know I shouldn't have interrupted and jumped in like that, but I couldn't just let her get away with that."

He wrapped one arm around the back of her neck and pulled her close, kissing her forehead. "Let's get some lunch. Marcus, you up for a quick bite?"

"I have Megan and Zach with me today." He jerked his thumb over his shoulder at the two preteens running around the parking lot.

"Why don't you bring them along?" Addie didn't hesitate to ask.

Marcus took them up on the offer, and they had lunch at a local diner. The kids kept everyone laughing, and Declan seemed completely relaxed, despite the episode after church with the nasty Mrs. Miller.

That awful woman had made Addie's blood boil in two seconds flat. The nerve of that old hag! She couldn't get over it. Declan was right when he said hate spreads easily.

Declan had been an adult pursuing a career—an honorable career at that. She doubted his grandparents had faulted him for his life choices. In fact, he had made plenty of good choices that now made up the wonderful man that she knew today.

He had been talkative and friendly at lunch. Quite a few people had approached their table to say quick greetings to either Declan, Marcus, or both, and he had greeted everyone with a genuine smile and sometimes a hearty hug.

When they pulled into the driveway at his house after church, he confessed that she had in fact helped him today, and he would love to keep going to church together. She had been so excited, she threw her arms around him and kissed him soundly.

She had to admit, it was flattering to hear that he drew strength from her presence. Her cheeks warmed and her feet itched to do a little happy dance accompanied by a girlish squeal. No one had ever made her feel needed and important until Declan.

In her excitement, she hadn't heard his phone ringing at first. "Sorry. Let me get this. I think I know what this is about."

She waved him to answer and sat back in her seat.

"Hello." He put the call on speaker for her to hear and gave her a playful grin.

"Hey, Dec. Who was that foxy lady I saw you with at church today?" a sweet feminine voice crooned on the other side of the call.

"Why are you even asking? I'm sure you've heard all about Addie by now." Declan was smiling, and she couldn't help but notice that he seemed very familiar with the woman calling. There was no hesitation, no shyness, no uncomfortable stuttering.

"Well, yeah, but I want the details from you too. Just save it. I'm almost at your house."

He sighed. "You know, you and your brother should learn how to give a heads-up. Five minutes doesn't count."

"Declan King, are you saying I'm not welcome?" The woman sounded offended.

"Of course, you're welcome. I'd just appreciate a warning. Send a flare, a carrier pigeon, just something."

"Mwah," the woman imitated the sound of an exaggerated kiss and the call went dead.

He laughed as he stuck the phone back in his pocket. "That was Sissy."

"You have a sister?" This was news. Never once had she heard him mention a sibling.

"No. She's Dakota's sister, but everyone calls her Sissy. She just found out about us, and she likes to have her nose in everyone's business. She wants to check in, but don't worry. She'll love you."

"Really?" Addie hadn't had a female friend in years, but the women she worked with were quickly becoming close friends. It was always nice to meet someone new.

Declan laughed. "Sissy doesn't meet a stranger. She'll have you under her wing in no time. She's loyal and a genuinely good person. You'll get along just fine, I'm sure." He kissed the top of her head gently as they mounted the porch stairs.

She ran her fingernail along her lips to keep from biting it. "You seemed very... close with Sissy."

He gave a playful huff. "I've known her my whole life, and she's always understood what's wrong with me. I've chosen my friends carefully over the years, but Sissy was just always there." He threw his keys onto the small table beside the door. "Some people are easier to be around than others. I think it has to do with how aware the other person is about my problem. There's a difference in Libby who is outgoing and pushy and Sissy who is assertive but understanding."

He sat down heavily on the couch and she took a seat beside him. "Sissy never pitied me, and she never pushed me either."

"I see. I think I get it." She smiled and linked her fingers with his.

"You know you're different from anyone I've ever met. I've never been able to talk to someone as easily as I can with you. I've only been able to be myself with maybe a dozen people I've ever known, and those friendships took years."

She squeezed his hand and her smile grew even larger. "Looks like things are changing for both of us."

CHAPTER EIGHTEEN

Adeline

Declan was right. Sissy was a walking, talking good time, and Addie loved her from the moment they met. The two were kindred spirits and took to each other immediately.

Sissy had silky black hair and tan skin like Dakota. The resemblance was startling. Declan had told her that Sissy was married to Ian's brother, Tyler, who had stitched Declan up on the first night they met but had failed to mention that Sissy was pregnant.

When Declan got the impression he was the odd man out, he told the girls he was going to make a trip to take some of the boxes they had packed up from his grandparents' house to the church. Once the women were alone, the conversation flowed, and Addie was amazed at how much she had missed female companionship.

Addie didn't hide her fascination with the pregnancy. She had never been around someone who was pregnant before, and it turned out she knew nothing about pregnancy and babies.

"So, when are you due?"

"Mid-October, but I'm shooting for October 10th. How cool would that be to have a 1010 birthday?" Addie agreed that would be a really cool birth date.

"What's it like being pregnant?" It was a general question, but she didn't know how to narrow it down. She wanted to know everything.

Sissy eased into a more relaxed position on the couch. Addie was painting Sissy's toenails a glossy shade of baby pink in honor of her daughter-to-be. Sissy said she had been carrying the polish around in her purse until she could find someone to help her paint them now that she couldn't bend over to reach her toes.

"It sounds a little silly, but I feel like this is my purpose in life. I feel like being pregnant is my natural state. It just feels right. Sure, you hear horror stories all the time about difficult pregnancies, but mine has been a breeze. I feel like I'm at my peak, I'm my best self. I've never been happier, but I'm sure that's the hormones talking."

Sissy made pregnancy sound like a walk in the park, and she didn't seem even the slightest bit scared. Even thinking about pregnancy and labor almost paralyzed Addie with fear, but that may have been the fear of the unknown talking. The more Sissy talked about it, the more her heart opened to the idea that maybe kids could be a part of her future.

"Does it ease your mind that your husband is a doctor?" she asked.

"Not really. Tyler is a general practitioner. Sure, he knows about pregnancy and delivery, but it's not his forte. If anything, he makes me a little crazy. I'm laid back, and I have no problem going with the flow. Tyler has been worried sick, and he panics about every little thing. We've always balanced each other out in life, but we are an example of opposites when it comes to this pregnancy. I'm carefree, and he is serious and rational. He makes me think twice about things I would brush off, and I help him find his control when he is losing his mind in fear."

Sissy and Tyler seemed to have it all figured out. She knew she was getting the abbreviated version of their relationship, but she could see Sissy's happiness when she talked about Tyler. They completed each other, and isn't that what everyone was looking for in a partner? A completion of his or her existing self? Sissy and Tyler didn't change each other but found their connection in the middle of their extremes. Maybe opposites did attract.

"You ever think about having kids?" Sissy's question pulled her from her train of thought.

"Not until now. It hasn't ever seemed like a possibility for me. I was in a bad relationship, and I knew bringing a child into that dynamic wasn't a good idea."

"You wouldn't believe how much it means to have the right person standing next to you through all of this. I couldn't imagine having a baby with anyone but Tyler. He's been my rock, and he's going to be the best dad." Sissy's voice cracked on the last word, and she wiped a stray tear from her cheek. "Sorry. It's the hormones. I swear I'm usually a tough cookie."

She picked up Sissy's hand and gave it a slight squeeze. "You really know how to make a woman question her life plan."

Sissy gave a deep laugh from her constricted throat. "You planning to tame the strong silent one?"

"I don't necessarily want to tame him. I don't think he needs that, and I don't want it. I like him the way he is." Now she couldn't look at Sissy as her blush grew.

"Oooooo you dooooo like him. Like, you like him a lot. Girl, you got it bad."

"Well, do you blame me? What's not to like?" she said defensively.

"You're right. He really is a great guy. He and Dakota have been friends since they were kids, so I grew up with him. Some people are just inherently good, and Declan is one of them. He just has a problem opening up to people. Half the time he doesn't even want to greet and shake hands with people. He's just closed off. It's his nature, but he seemed really comfortable with you." Sissy gave a playful wink. "I had already planned to tease him about you. What can I say, it's my sisterly duty."

"Speaking of, is Sissy your real name?" Addie asked casually.

"Goodness, no. It's Melanie, but Dakota was about two and a half years old when I was born and couldn't say my name. You've seen it before. Some stranger is trying to be nice and engage the kids so she asks the older sibling 'Well, who is this?' Dakota would proudly tell them all 'This is Sissy,' so that's what everyone called me. Now, very few people remember my real name."

"That is the cutest story. Does it bother you that people don't use your real name?" she asked, completely immersed in Sissy's life story.

"Nah, it's all I've known." Sissy gave a slight shrug and rubbed her swollen belly.

She finished up the finishing touches on Sissy's toenail polish and cleaned up the mess.

"So are the two of you officially in a relationship?" Sissy was gushing for the details.

"He introduced me as his girlfriend at church today, and we were sort of in the middle of discussing our true relationship status when the drive-by happened."

"I heard about that. How awful. I trust Jake, so I'm sure he's working hard to find that guy." Then Sissy clapped in delight. "I'm so happy for you both. Really, we were all starting to worry that Declan wouldn't find anyone he could be himself with, you know? He's not like other people. It's difficult for him to connect with anyone. I'm really glad he's found that with you."

Addie was glad too. As much as Sissy believed she was helping Declan, he was helping her just as much. They were learning to grow together, and that was more than she ever could have imagined for herself in a relationship.

"He just jumped into my life and... saved me." He had saved her in more ways than one. He saved her life when he defended her from Jason and rescued her soul when he helped her get back her relationship with God.

Sissy stretched again. "Believe it or not, you're not the first life he has saved."

"What do you mean?"

Sissy tugged at the hem of her shirt as she thought about how to begin. "Did Declan tell you that Dakota has a problem?"

"He mentioned alcohol once."

Sissy nodded. "Right. Well, a few years ago, Declan was stationed at Fort Hood in Texas when he got a late-night call from Dakota. My stupid brother had been drinking all night and ran his truck into a ditch." Sissy sucked in a shaky breath. "I'll never know if he did it on purpose or if he wrecked because he had been drinking. I'll never ask him because I'm afraid to know the answer."

Addie couldn't imagine what that kind of struggle must be like for Dakota, as well as the people who loved him. She kept silent as Sissy composed herself to remember the horrifying night.

"Kota knew he was a dead man, but he called Declan. I think he knew Declan was the only one who couldn't come after him, and he just didn't want to die alone. He should have known better. Declan found the first person with a cell phone in the middle of the night and called me. Told me to call the police and start looking for him. Declan couldn't tell where he had wrecked, but he mentioned a place where Dakota had been earlier in the night."

Sissy cradled her stomach and took another deep breath. "I called 911 and they sent someone looking for him, but I also called everyone I knew and had them driving the roads looking for his Bronco in a ditch. I finally found him about an hour later. He was unconscious from all the blood he lost, but he was alive."

Sissy grabbed Addie's hand and squeezed. "You see, if Declan hadn't called so quickly, I would have lost my brother that night. I owe him so much for what he has done for our family. Dakota's addiction is hard on all of us, but Declan hasn't ever turned his back on his friend. Not once. That kind of loyalty is admirable."

"It really is." Addie shouldn't have been surprised by Sissy's story. It was so like Declan to go above and beyond for others.

A few minutes later, Declan returned from his errand, and Addie couldn't help looking at him with reverence. "I missed you."

"I missed you too." He didn't make fun of her for missing him when he had only been gone for less than an hour. After hearing Sissy's story of almost losing her brother, she was reminded that time was precious and fragile.

Sissy looked at her watch. "I really need to get going. I promised Tyler I would make his favorite dinner if he would rub my feet while I watch soap operas."

"Tell him to call me. We should all get together sometime." Declan gave Sissy a side hug as he navigated around her large belly.

"That would be awesome. By the way, how's the scratch?"

Declan brushed her off. "I'm good as new, thanks to Tyler."

"I know. He's pretty handy to have around sometimes." She smiled with a look of pride as she waved good-bye. "Great meeting you, Addie. We're definitely hanging out soon."

Addie couldn't believe the turn her life had taken in such a short time. With school, work, helping Declan, and now her new friends, her days were filled with joy.

CHAPTER NINETEEN

Adeline

Declan dropped Addie off at The Line a few minutes before she and Karen had agreed to meet, but her aunt was already seated and working on a cup of coffee while reading the local newspaper.

The Line was a diner located on the Cherokee County line, and their food was second to none. It had quickly become Addie's favorite lunch stop.

"Hey, am I late? I thought we said noon? Have you been here long?" She hated being late, and keeping someone waiting was the worst.

"Oh, no. I'm just conditioned to wake up with the sun, so I ran some errands around town this morning and decided to take a minute to myself to browse the news." Karen stood to hug her with a smile on her face to light up the night. "You look great, honey. I have to say I think the Georgia air is doing wonders for you."

As they took their seats, she didn't want to tell Karen that it was more than the air or the place. It was the people and the life she was living here. It was the life she *could* have here if things went the right way.

"I know. Thank you for taking me in when I needed help. I wouldn't be here and happy without you." She would be forever grateful for this woman and silently hoped she would find a way to repay her kindness one day. She hadn't been spending much time at home lately between work, school, and spending time with Declan.

"I love you. You've always been so good to me, and you took me in when you didn't have to," Addie said with sincerity.

Karen reached for her hand over the table. "I love you too. I love you like you're my own. Butch and I never had kids, but I was lucky enough to be able to teach half the people in this town at some point in time. I loved watching them grow and learn and become the adults they were meant to be, but you've been the most inspiring. Your transformation has been quick and full in these past few months. I'm incredibly proud of you, and your parents would be too."

Her parents. She had pushed all thoughts of them away for so long, fearing they would be disappointed in how her life had turned out if they were here to see her. She had felt like a failure to them for so long while she wasted her days away being controlled by Jason.

Now, maybe she could entertain the thought of making a life for herself that they would have loved to see. What if she could finally have a job she enjoyed, friends she cared about, and a family she loved.

A family? She hadn't dared dream of a family for herself in years. When her parents had been alive, she had wanted that more than anything. She wanted what they had given her, and it consumed her motivations more than college or a career.

The bell above the door gave a greeting ring that pulled her attention, and she watched as Marcus walked in with a young boy around nine and another boy who looked to be high school age behind him. He gave her a discreet nod before making his way to an empty booth not fifteen feet away from her.

"Is that your eagle eye for the day?" Karen asked knowingly.

Addie laughed. "They do watch out for me when they're around, but they keep their distance."

"I know, honey. I'm glad he's here. How are things going with Declan?"

She had asked it so casually, but the answer felt anything but casual. She felt so much for him, it couldn't be summarized into a quick response.

"He's been... wonderful. He takes this problem I'm having very seriously, and he doesn't make me feel bad for practically barging into his life with my baggage. And we're almost finished cleaning up his grandparents' house."

"Oh, come on. Can I at least have some *real* girl talk? Are you hitting things off yet?" She sounded as excited as a school girl with gossip.

Addie laughed. "Actually, we are. We were both a little hesitant at first. I've been worried about making another colossal relationship mistake, and he has a hard time opening up. I think we had all the relationship anxiety we can handle in the beginning between the two of us."

"Don't all couples have their doubts in the beginning? You can't hold back from having a relationship because you had a bad one in the past, and you shouldn't give up before it starts just because it *could* eventually end." Karen gave her a look that said *You're smarter than this*.

"I'm a complete newbie at this relationship thing."

"I'm not worried about that. When two people have a healthy connection, they find ways to let each other know how they feel. You may not have the easiest relationship in the beginning, but sometimes it gets easier as you become comfortable together."

She smiled and hope sprang up in her chest. Sure, she and Declan had tiptoed around each other at times, but she knew he cared for her. She didn't have to wonder anymore. He had made his feelings known that he didn't want to continue the fake aspect of the relationship, and that was a promising start.

"I think you're absolutely right. I really believe this could work out between us… if we could settle whatever this is with Jason."

She hated that Jason put a damper on all of the good things in her life. Why couldn't he just move on and leave her alone to go about her own business?

Because he needs to control you.

She shook her head to erase the thought. She couldn't stand to think about the way he had kept her dimmed and drained for so long.

"The problem with Jason will work itself out. Maybe he will give up and move on."

Karen was so optimistic that she almost allowed herself to consider the possibility.

She looked to Marcus to find him scanning the restaurant. Always keeping an eye out for anyone who could be interested in what she was doing. Always searching for whoever could be hunting her. She silently wondered if Jason would ever exit her life quietly.

"I hope you're right, Karen."

They ordered lunch and she filled her aunt in on the plans to renovate the salon soon. Her boss, Helen, had assured her that she would still have a job when the salon reopened. She was almost grateful for the break. Her midterms were coming up at school, and she could use the extra off hours to study.

When their plates were cleared, Karen gave Addie a ride back to work. She promised she would be home right after work tonight. She had a test next week, and she needed to cram as much as she could over the weekend.

Fridays at the salon were always busy, and Addie jumped back into the fray after lunch, trying to keep up with the waiting customers and the needs of the stylists, while Marcus sat in a brown padded seat against the glass storefront watching her. Declan had some work to do this evening, so Marcus had agreed to come in for a trim and wait around to be her ride home.

At least that was the story they told Amy. She hated telling half-truths when she felt like Amy was turning into a real friend. She knew how *not* to start a good friendship, and she was doing just that.

She stole another glance at Marcus, but his attention was focused on the quiet street. Once again, she felt the pang of shame that her problems were interfering with so many lives. They had all become a little more cautious since Jason's last stunt.

"Are you sure you wouldn't rather sit by Amy's station? I know the sun is baking you by that window."

Addie hated that he always sat by the window, and Declan sat there too when he came by the salon. She knew they chose that place because they had a better view of the store and the street outside, but it was summer, and he was certainly scorching by the window. The A/C in the salon wasn't powerful enough to keep up in the summer months.

"I'm fine." He was short and to the point as he brushed her off like she was being a mother hen.

It was ten minutes until closing when she heard the bell above the door chime. She knew they didn't have any more appointments booked for the day, so it must be a walk-in. Amy rolled her eyes, huffed a grunt, and said, "Send 'em to me," before dramatically pushing herself out of her styling chair to get ready for the client.

She knew how Amy felt. She was tired herself, and her feet were screaming after the long work day. As much as she wanted to blow this popsicle stand, she tried to adopt the mindset that catering to the customer's needs is smart business.

She turned the corner into the front waiting area, and her heart stopped. Jason stood right inside the door. Marcus was seething, standing mere inches from Jason, clenching and unclenching his fists at his side in an effort to control himself.

"What are you doing here?" Marcus said, and even Addie couldn't help but be intimidated by him.

"I'm getting a haircut. Is that a problem?" Jason was being cheeky. He turned to her and glared as he chastised her, "You should really consider getting a better greeter."

Amy rounded the corner and gave everyone a stern look that said *Don't scare away the business*. "What's going on out here?"

Jason let his eyes blatantly look her up and down before speaking. "Not a thing, dollface." He reached out his hand to her in greeting. "I'm Jason, Adeline's ex-boyfriend. Good to meet you." He was smiling at Amy now, but even Amy could see that his heart wasn't in it.

"Oh, really? She never mentioned you." Amy gave Addie a *What in the world is going on* look and tugged her hand from Jason's grasp.

"That's a blow to the ego. We were together for years. I thought I had made quite a big impression on her." He turned to look at Addie again, assessing her for the bruises he had inflicted a few weeks ago, and she could see that Marcus was losing his patience.

Apparently, Amy noticed too. "If you'll follow me this way, I'll get you set up. Just a trim today?"

Jason's brown hair was shaggy and unkempt, and he ran his fingers through it as he thought. "That sounds wonderful, doll. How about we get rid of the length and shape it up on top? I've let things get out of control lately, but it looks like it's time to buckle down."

Addie didn't miss the double meaning, and she was having trouble breathing. Marcus was a statue beside her, only a breath away but hard as stone. She could feel the anger radiating from him. She turned to him and her mouth opened, but no words came out.

When Marcus spoke, he seemed more in control than she had anticipated. "I won't let him hurt you." He never took his eyes off Jason who was making himself comfortable in Amy's salon chair.

Addie and Marcus moved around the corner, far enough away to not be considered lurking but still close enough to hear the conversation between Jason and Amy.

"So, Adeline really hasn't mentioned me?" Jason was fishing for dirt on her, and part of her was grateful that he had come in so late in the day. Amy wouldn't be in a very talkative mood if she was ready to get out of there.

"Nope. Addie doesn't talk much about her life before she came here. In fact, I don't think she's ever mentioned to me where she is from."

"You call her Addie? She has always gone by Adeline. Hm, that's strange, don't you think? Sounds like she's hiding something." He was planting the seeds of doubt in Amy's mind, and she hoped with all her heart that Amy was loyal enough to her to see through it.

"Everyone has a past. Not everyone wants to announce theirs to the world." Addie gave a sigh of relief that Amy had cut him off so quickly, and she made a mental note to thank her later.

She turned to Marcus and whispered, "What do we do?" She sounded only slightly panicked. Having no-nonsense Marcus beside her gave her more strength than she realized.

"Nothing. Don't give in to him. I got a message to Declan and Jake. Jake can arrest him since he has a warrant on his head. Hopefully, one of them can get someone here before Amy finishes."

Marcus had no obligation to her, yet here he was taking charge and helping her without question.

Marcus merely stood by her, calming her and assuring her in his own way until Amy was finished with Jason. Addie was completely composed as she positioned herself at the checkout desk.

"Twenty dollars," Addie said in a deadpan voice.

"Here I am giving you money again, just like old times." Jason sneered and leaned in to whisper so that only she could hear. "I hate it just as much now as I did then."

Somehow, having Marcus here and knowing Declan would be here soon gave her more courage than she had ever known, and seeing Jason here infuriated her. Of course, Jason knew where she worked. He had attacked her in the alley, but she was a different person now. She was stronger and more determined than ever to be a woman who would never back down to someone like Jason.

She steadied herself, stood tall, and looked Jason in the eye with a smile. "Actually, you took my money, and I never saw a fraction of it. You can keep your money. I don't want it." The evenness of her voice surprised her, but she saw the complete shock on Jason's face.

He stood still for one heartbeat with the money hanging from his fingers before his smile melted and was replaced by the face of hatred. "Listen here, you ungrateful—"

"That's enough." Marcus stepped behind him, almost herding him toward the door, but Jason resisted.

Her ex's eyes were narrowed and cold as he spat, "I own you, and this little stunt you're pulling is only making things worse for you. Got it?" His hand had fisted around the money as he spoke.

She would never know if Jason had more to say. Marcus was behind him in an instant with the back of his shirt balled into his fist as he pulled Jason away from her. "That's it. You don't have any business talking to her that way."

Jason kept his eyes on her as he feebly fought to free himself from Marcus' grasp. Once Marcus let him go, Jason stalked for the door.

Jason stopped with his hands on the door. "Don't worry. I'm not finished," he snarled at Marcus as he turned away and strode down the sidewalk as if nothing had happened.

Marcus rubbed his hands together before propping them against the checkout desk as if he was completely in control. He leveled her with a serious stare. "I'm sorry. I know we were supposed to keep him here, but I forgot all about that when he came at you. He's just trying to scare you."

"I know. I'm fine." Really, she was. Her heart was threatening to burst from her chest, but she felt strong. Maybe it was just the adrenaline from the confrontation, but she felt brave. She wasn't foolish enough to believe it would last. The shock would hit her soon, and she would fall apart.

She gave Marcus the best smile she could manage and said, "Thank you for that."

His lip twitched into a lazy smile that lasted only a blink. "No problem."

Amy interrupted them with her hands on her hips. "All right. Who is gonna tell me what just happened?"

The bell on the door chimed and Declan burst through the door with pounding footfalls in his heavy boots. "Where's Addie? Where is he?"

Marcus replied as he texted furiously on his phone, "Gone. Jake will keep looking for him. I don't think he could have gotten far."

Declan gripped his hair at the roots before throwing his fists down by his sides and directing all his flaming attention on Addie. "Are you all right?"

"I'm fine. Really, I'm all right." She was for now, at least. She was unsure of any delayed reaction she may experience, but she was fine for the moment.

"Good." He deflated slightly as the relief washed over him and he strode to her in two long steps to bring her into his arms. All was right in the world in this moment. She was with Declan, and everything felt right as butterflies danced in her stomach.

Declan was showing her how much he cared about her safety, how much she meant to him. Just as he had from the beginning. He cupped her head and folded her into his body in consolation as he whispered, "What happened?"

Amy was tired of being ignored. "Yeah, what just happened?"

Addie pulled slightly from him and looked at Marcus for his input, but he shrugged and deferred the storytelling to her. She told Declan of Jason's arrival, his questioning Amy, and his outburst at the checkout counter.

Marcus added, "And she pretty much told him to shove it."

Declan turned to her with an uninhibited smile. "I'm not gonna lie, I'm incredibly proud of you right now. I would pay good money to have seen that."

"Okay, now please tell me the significance of his visit. Why is it such a big deal, other than the guy was creepy?" Amy was still confused.

Addie looked at her friend and understood the frustration. The only reason she hadn't told Amy about Jason before was because she was embarrassed.

"Jason *is* my ex-boyfriend. When I came here two months ago, I was running from him. He pretty much kept me locked up for years, stole all of my money, and lied to me about his job. I thought he was in marketing when really he was selling drugs. He has warrants out for his arrest, and I didn't even know it. I left him without warning when I found out. He never physically abused me until I ran." Her voice faltered at the end, and Amy quickly closed the gap between them to grab her into a back-breaking hug.

"I'm so sorry. I wish I had known. I would have kicked him out from the beginning."

"I wouldn't have asked you to do that, Amy. Actually, we were trying to keep him here until a deputy could get here to arrest him. He has warrants out for his arrest."

Amy looked at Declan. "How did you get caught in the middle of all this?"

Declan locked eyes with her as he spoke, "Addie's aunt and uncle asked me to keep an eye out for her a while back, and things just escalated between us after we met."

Addie hated that her problem had reared its ugly head once again. "I'm sorry about all of this. I don't want you to feel obligated to help me."

Declan pulled her to him. "I've never felt obligated to care for you or stand beside you. I want to be here."

And there it was. He had twisted the words his father had spoken that had cut him to the core as a teenager and made them a vow instead of a hateful memory. He had no real responsibility to her, and he was letting her know it. He was here because he cared, because he wanted to be here.

"Thank you." It was all she could manage. Her mind was spinning and her vision blurred with unshed tears.

Amy grabbed her hand, getting her attention. "You two should go. I'll wrap things up here."

Declan shook his head. "Sorry. Can't do that. I'm not leaving you here alone after Jason made an appearance. Let us help you close up, and we can all leave at the same time." She shouldn't be surprised by Declan's gentlemanly ways anymore, but her heart warmed to him even more.

Marcus offered, "I'll stay and help Amy. You two can go on."

"Amy, is that all right with you?" Declan asked.

"That would be great. Thank you. I'm not feeling as comfortable closing up alone after that story." She sounded genuinely affected.

"Don't let her take out the trash alone," Addie said to Marcus in an effort to ease the tension as she playfully poked his chest with one finger.

Declan's face was stern as he pulled her into a back-breaking hug. "Right. Actually, y'all need to set up a buddy system for taking out the trash on days that I'm not here." He looked at Amy as if it was her job to make sure the women around here used proper caution.

"You got it, boss." She gave him a wink as she turned to start closing the shop.

Addie walked with Declan in the fading twilight of the sidewalk outside the salon a few minutes later, and she felt a sense of extra fortification knowing that Amy would be by her side through this too. Her circle of trust was growing, and she was glad. Jason had given her every reason to doubt the motives for honesty and trustworthiness in others, but she wasn't going to let the mistakes of one horrible person keep her from letting people in.

Suddenly, Declan pulled her to him so their bodies were flush, and she gave him a hooded stare. He tightened his hold on her, and her ribs were screaming for release as he eased up and stroked her hair. "It kills me every time I think about him being close to you."

She reciprocated the hug and held him tight. "I know. It scares me too, but we made it through another encounter. Thanks for rushing in like a white knight again." She chuckled, but he continued to hold her tight.

After a few more moments of holding each other on the busy sidewalk, she asked, "Will you take me home, and maybe stay with me for a while. I'm sure Karen made dinner, and I'm not ready to be away from you yet."

He pulled away from her and nodded as he guided her toward his truck. "Of course. I'm not ready to let you go either."

CHAPTER TWENTY

Declan

Declan and Addie spent the day together after her test the next week, but neither of them had any plans for the day. They decided to take some time off from cleaning at his grandparents' house, since they were almost finished and had been working in every spare minute for weeks.

They spent the late morning watching movies and eating cinnamon rolls, but when afternoon rolled around, he told Addie he needed to make some phone calls. She offered to make lunch while he tended to business.

His previously made plans to take her to dinner one day this past weekend evaporated with the run-in with Jason, and he understood why she wanted to stay in. Jason's eyes were everywhere, and the more he saw her, the more vulnerable she felt.

He was sitting at the table in the kitchen with his laptop open in front of him and Jake talking away on speakerphone beside him, but the only thing he could focus on was Addie standing at the stove as she cooked.

She was beautiful, and he was distracted by her more often than not. He tried to pull himself into the conversation with Jake, but his heart wasn't in it.

There was another thought he couldn't push from his mind. He wasn't scared of Jason, but he was scared of the fact that Jason wanted to take Addie from him. He wouldn't let it happen. His mind was firm. The run-in with Jason had lit a fire under him, but the seeds of *what if* had seeped into his mind.

Jason's reappearance had shaken him to the core. If he was being honest, he was terrified. He had just found her, and his blood ran cold when he thought of the things that Jason wanted to do to her. He couldn't stomach a life without her light, her happiness, her warm presence.

He had filled Jake in on the meeting with Jason, and Jake was just as shaken as he was. Jake had been torn up that he didn't have the manpower to send someone for Jason at the salon quickly enough.

"I hate being so short staffed. Our budget is skin tight, and we need about five more deputies. We just can't afford it. Stuff like this makes me feel like we'll never get out of this hole. We should be able to be everywhere we are needed in a moment's notice."

Jake was beating himself up, but Declan had known it was a long shot they would be able to catch him at the salon. He had been too late himself. He pinched the bridge of his nose in an attempt to ease the tension headache he felt pricking at his eyes. "He was only there for about ten minutes tops. You didn't have a big window of time."

"Still, I hate it when anything gets past us." Jake blew a deep breath into the receiver.

Declan had him on speakerphone, and Addie turned around to sit at the table with him. "Declan is right. You're doing your best, and we appreciate everything you do. Don't beat yourself up about it."

Did she know her voice was heavenly? He wanted to bottle it up and save it for all the times when things looked bad. She was a cooling balm to any sore situation. Did she know that she was his motivation in everything? From catching Jason to getting his life together to building a future, she was in the center of every thought driving him forward. He felt like he had a purpose when she was around.

"Thanks again, Jake. We'll keep you posted."

He disconnected the call, and she stood to check on the jambalaya she was making. She was cooking in his kitchen as if she owned the place, and he couldn't help but wish to keep her in this moment for as long as possible.

She continued cooking and seemed to have calmed slightly with the necessity of a task in front of her, but he wanted her to be at peace. He wanted to give her unending peace and protection. A life of contentment sounded like something she would want, but he wanted to give her more than that. He wanted to give her a life of adventure, purpose, and passion. He wanted to give her all the things she wanted, and all the things she had given him—hope, desire, motivation.

He stood before he could lose his nerve and went to her. His skin buzzed and his heart hammered like a machine gun, but this wasn't a battle, this was a peace treaty. Her back was still turned to him as she grabbed the dishes from the cabinets and placed them beside the finished jambalaya.

She turned to him with a look of confusion just as he reached her, and he slowly advanced toward her until the small of her back met the counter and trapped her with his arms propped on either side of her body. He could feel her breath on his face, and she gently placed her hands on his chest but didn't push as he looked deep into her eyes, saying more in a look than he could with words.

He had never been good at expressing himself in words, but he felt like most communication that he had with Addie happened without them. She had a way of conveying feelings with her touch instead of words. There was something special about spending time with someone where no words are needed. Actions and silence working together to say the things that were too precious to be brought to air.

Before his mind had time to react, his body was leaning in to her. He stopped so close to her lips that one breath could connect them. He ran one hand up to her neck before pulling her in, taking her mouth in a passionate rush that was the most intimate kiss he had ever been a part of, and he still wanted more of her. He would never have enough of her.

When their kiss broke, her hands were still on his chest, and she let them drop to the healing wound across his lower ribs. Her face lost its playfulness, and she leaned down to pull his T-shirt up and get a better look. When she gently brushed her fingers over the scar, he would have sworn she hadn't touched him if he hadn't watched her delicate fingertips make contact with his skin. He hadn't felt a thing. When she was satisfied with her appraisal, she straightened and met his gaze. "How does it feel?"

"Much better. It's really not more than a scratch."

She rolled her eyes and gave him a mischievous smile. "Right. I forgot you're Mr. Tough Guy."

"Nah. I've just had worse injuries. This is nothing, really." There were a few injuries he certainly wished he didn't remember. His blood ran cold at the memories of the more painful ones.

She ducked her head and shied away from the topic of conversation. He tended to avoid talking about his time in the Army. Not much of it came into play in his daily life anymore, and he was looking forward, not back.

"I was in the Army for eight years. I didn't shy away from the fire, so I was bound to get burned." He paused to look her in the eyes. He was letting her know it was all right to ask about them.

He lifted her hand in his and gently placed it on a particularly gruesome scar on his right side. "This was a bullet. I was incredibly lucky that it only grazed me. Two other people who were close by didn't make it. I was miles away from any place that could have given me the medical attention I needed, and I lost a lot of blood. My friend carried me the last mile after I passed out. The wound was filthy, and I was hospitalized for weeks."

He moved her hand to the long scar that bisected his elbow without making eye contact with her. He couldn't look at her while he did this.

"We were on a night raid when the building I was standing next to blew up. I was thrown back in the explosion and my elbow must have connected with something hard enough to shatter it. Two of my friends dug me out of the debris, but I don't remember much of it. I had a concussion, and I was in and out of it for the better part of a week. I had two surgeries on the elbow, but it still isn't the way it used to be. It never will be."

She had listened intently, and he warily turned to face her. Her eyes were only slightly glassy, and she grazed her fingers over the mangled scar on his side.

"Your scars are beautiful. You're telling me horror stories, but I can see you in front of me now. You're not scaring me away with your nightmares. You're telling me stories of how you survived. You're telling me of how you made it through it all, and you lived to tell me about it." She moved her gaze and her hand to the long scar that ran the length of his elbow. "I'm seeing a happy ending."

He raised her chin to force her eyes to his. "I love your mind. You have a unique way of seeing things that is selectively beautiful and optimistic." He placed a chaste kiss on her forehead and gathered her into a bear hug that may have been a little too snug.

When he released her, she was all smiles and the weight of his revelations had dissipated. He loved that she didn't look at him with pity or horror when he had to confess things that were unpleasant to think about. She knew how to make him feel at ease sharing every part of himself with her.

"How about we pick up those self-defense lessons again?" He had been slowly showing her how to protect herself in the event that Jason came around while he wasn't there to protect her.

"That sounds great. I'd feel better with another lesson under my belt."

After lunch they sauntered into the front yard while Reaper circled Addie's legs like a satellite. She jumped from side to side, toying with the German Shepherd before throwing a tennis ball across the yard.

"You know I have to put him up, right?" Reaper didn't take too kindly to Declan's pretend advances on Addie.

"I know. I'll lead him in when he gets back with the ball." He loved seeing her full of life and excitement. It twisted his heart that she had been caged for so long.

When Reaper was locked inside, he went over the basics they had discussed in their previous lessons. From what he had observed, Addie was a quick learner when it came to most anything.

She encouraged his friends to talk about the things they loved or their jobs, and she absorbed every word they gave her. She peppered them with questions until she felt she had at least a crude understanding of the subject. She hadn't been able to get much out of Marcus yet, but she was still working on him.

Brian had opened up about his love of music and the gigs he played at the local hangouts. She had been so enraptured with his passion that he had offered to teach her to play guitar. It wasn't a surprise when he had confided to Declan that she was musically gifted.

She talked business with Ian and Dakota, who both had mentioned innovative ideas she had given them. She had a unique way of looking at all sides to find unlikely solutions to problems.

He was glad she had quickly picked up the concepts of gun safety and usage. When she took to those lessons so well, he decided she may need some basic knowledge of knife wielding, since that was the only weapon he had seen Jason actually use.

She had felt comfortable with the blade in no time, and they agreed that she should carry it when she wasn't with him. She didn't have a permit to carry a gun, so that was only for emergency use at his house. They ran through a few basic maneuvers for the knife from time to time, outside of their official lessons.

They spent the majority of their time working on hand-to-hand combat. Of course, all three skills would require many hours of practice, but this one required more honing, since she hadn't taken much stock in physical exercise or athletics in a while. It helped that she was naturally athletic, but she was a bit clumsy.

After a few hours of their instruction, she leaned over panting with her hands on her knees. "I'm sorry. I feel like I'm tripping over my own feet."

Her brunette hair was pulled back into a bouncing ponytail and sweat beads had formed on her brow.

"You've done an amazing job today." He was panting too, but Addie tended to steal his breath. "You're learning quickly."

"I have an awesome teacher. Haven't you heard?" He loved it when she playfully complimented him. Sometimes, he wondered how they could be so well suited for each other.

"How did I get so lucky?" he breathed on a whisper. He hadn't meant to wonder out loud, but he wasn't sorry he had.

"I'm the lucky one. I'm lucky to be saved by you. I'm lucky to be protected by you…" She turned to him and ran her fingers through his beard. "I'm lucky… in all the ways I never knew I could be."

He kissed her and hoped she heard all of the unspoken words and the silent reverence that wouldn't be contained any longer.

Declan's attention was drawn from their kiss quickly as he noticed a strange vehicle pulling into the driveway. He was instantly on high alert, since it could very well be Jason stopping in again uninvited. They were completely exposed in the middle of the front yard.

When the vehicle pulled farther into the gravel drive, he realized he knew just who was visiting, and this man was about as welcome as Jason.

He turned to Addie and said, "Wait here for just a minute please," in a tone that didn't allow for questions even when he was sure she had hundreds. He couldn't answer any of them right now. He had his own questions to be answered.

Declan's dad was well into his sixties now, with a weathered tan from years of hard labor. His weatherworn face sported a white goatee that had been brown the last time they had met.

The man made his way around the truck and met him in the yard. Declan approached the ghost head on. "I don't know what you want, but you won't find it here. It's best if you just leave now." His voice wasn't loud, but it was stern.

"I don't want anything from you, boy. I heard you were back in town, and I just wanted to talk. Can't you at least give me that?" The old man's tone wasn't pleading. It was entitled.

"No. I can't give you that. I'm a little busy, and you're not welcome here."

"I didn't know you were back in town, Dec."

"Who told you I was back?" He knew who had called his old man. He would bet that Mrs. Miller hadn't made it out of the church parking lot before calling him.

His dad had the decency to look ashamed. "Well, that ain't important."

"I said I'm busy," he said with finality as he turned back to Addie.

"Come on, Declan. You're gonna let some girl take precedence over your old man?" He gestured to her in the yard, and Declan briefly wondered why his dad had crossed that line he knew nothing about. He had never had any problems controlling his temper in the past. He tended to go with the flow, and his feathers didn't get ruffled often, but in one swift movement, he turned toward his dad and it happened in the blink of an eye. He closed the gap between them and grabbed the front of the older man's shirt into his fist.

His dad may have been more seasoned, but those prominent muscles in his father's arms meant nothing as he grabbed at Declan's fists. He had no doubt he could have the man on the ground and at his mercy in two seconds flat.

Declan's voice was full of fire as he locked eyes with the other man an inch from his nose. "Listen to me. That woman is my welcome future. You are my unwelcome past. You'd best find yourself in the pecking order around here in a hurry."

Declan threw the man from his grasp as quickly as if he had been burned. As his father tried to right himself quickly, Declan took a slow step forward and spat through gritted teeth, "Get off my property before I call the cops. You're not welcome here."

The man obliged and stomped back toward his vehicle with a glare before closing his truck door with a little too much force.

CHAPTER TWENTY - ONE

Adeline

When his father was out of sight, Declan made his way to Addie and picked up the unloaded gun they had been using for training. In the wake of his silence, the air felt thick. She didn't know what to say, so she kept quiet.

He entered the house, and he calmly returned the gun to its resting place on top of the bookshelf before addressing her without turning to look her way. "I'll take you home." His voice was emotionless. A part of her understood his need to be alone, and another part of her felt the sting of dismissal.

She grabbed her purse and tried to keep her mind from Declan and his isolation. She wanted to be there for him when he doubted himself or felt angry at the parent who had abandoned him. The sting of what his father had done to him was sure to be fresh in his mind right now, and he was shutting himself away instead of turning to her when the doubts came looking for him.

She shifted uncomfortably in the truck seat for a few minutes. She understood that people dealt with situations in different ways, but maybe he didn't know that leaning on her was an option. He had been dealing with anything and everything in his life alone for so long, maybe that was his default reaction.

She turned to him and whispered, "Do you want to talk about it?" His eyes were tired and lacked the spark she had come to love.

"No, I don't." There was too much finality in that retort, and she felt helpless.

"A-are you sure?"

He turned to her sharply. "I don't want to talk about it, Adeline."

Those words stung like a shot to the gut. Another dismissal, and he had used her full name, not the playful "Addie" she had come to love hearing. He was pushing her away. She could feel it, and her heart constricted with the loss.

"I just... I wanted you to know I'm here if you need me." She felt stupid and irrelevant now. How could things have gone wrong so easily? She didn't know how to navigate life situations in the dynamic of a relationship, but she felt like they should work together. She had told him she wanted the good and the bad with him, and he hadn't taken her words to heart.

When he finally spoke, the words were worse than she could have imagined. "I don't need anyone."

She stared at him without saying a word as he drove down the empty, tree-covered roads. He was going to leave her with those words, and there was nothing she could do about it. She found herself helpless and afraid again.

"Declan, don't you think you should give him a chance to..." She trailed off because she really didn't know what she had meant to say. She was pulling at strings that were falling away like broken spider webs.

He rounded on her and she recoiled out of instinct. His brows pulled together and his frown was morphing into a scowl as he spoke fast and furiously. "Every time you give someone a chance, that means they could die at any moment, leaving you gutted and alone. They could leave in the night without a word or a backward glance because they just didn't care about you like they biologically should."

He stared at the road ahead as he continued, opening himself to her like a bursting dam. "They could just wake up one morning and decide they don't love you the way you love them, and then who is the loser, again? I am." He stabbed a finger into his chest and willed her to feel his rage. "My track record for enticing people to stick around is the worst, so don't tell me this is a chance for a new beginning or some other mess. No, I don't think I should give him another chance. That's just a chance for a new ending, and I'm not up for another good-bye."

Now her shame and fear had mounted to the point of panic, but with that loss of control came her own anger. How could he push her away after all they had shared? How could he blame her for someone else's mistakes when she had made sure that their personal relationship wouldn't be affected by Jason's mistakes in her past?

"That's it? I don't get my own chance?" She halted her retreat and squared her shoulders toward him. "You're going to make me—no us, suffer for someone else's mistakes? We both have reasons to close ourselves off from the people who could hurt us. The difference between you and me is that I'm holding out for a hero and you've given up."

He was huffing in anger and his eyes were blazing, but she felt the fire now too as she continued. "I can't speak for you, but my way provides at least a chance of happiness. I don't *want* to be alone because it's all I've known. I want to be happy because it's what I *want* to know."

He pulled into the driveway at Karen and Butch's house, and she turned to him as she held the door handle to exit the truck. "I thought that once people like us found someone who loved us enough to stick around we would appreciate it more... because we know what it means when someone chooses to stay, when someone picks us." She leapt from the truck as fast as she could. She would not let him see her cry now.

Addie lay on the bed in her room staring at the ceiling trying to calm her tumultuous thoughts. Sure, couples were bound to have fights, but he had ended things with her *before* their first fight. She hadn't stood a chance against the war he was fighting inside himself. He was blinded by his hurt, and she was a necessary casualty to him.

When her heart had returned to a normal rhythm and she had let her body give in to the emotional toll the afternoon had taken, she rolled onto her side and closed her eyes. Maybe she would wake up and her fight with Declan would all be a bad dream.

She woke confused and hot as the evening sun streamed through the window of the bedroom. She stretched as her eyes adjusted to the light of the room.

Declan sat beside the bed in the small, ornate chair from her vanity. His elbows were propped on his knees and his hands hung loosely in front of him. Those blue eyes she loved so much were bloodshot and dull. She hated seeing him so broken, even after the things he said that had hurt her.

"I'm sorry." His voice was low and tired. "I'm so sorry." He moved his chair closer so he could take her hand. He held it firmly but gently as he looked at her—really looked at her—to convey all his meaning. "I was wrong, and you were right. I just didn't think to see it that way until you showed me."

He let his head rest on the hand he still held. She only hesitated a moment before running her hand through his hair. She felt the tension in his shoulders ease marginally as she stroked his hair reassuringly.

"I thought about what you said..." He raised his head to speak to her. "About my dad. I didn't handle the meeting very well, and you're right. I shouldn't have shut him out like that." He shook his head in shame.

"I've also thought about what you said about sticking together during the good times and the bad times. I don't know if I didn't believe it before or if I just didn't think I could believe it. Now, I really hope you meant it because I was a jerk and I wish I could take back everything I said because I wasn't mad at you. Not even a little bit. I was mad at him, and I foolishly took it out on you. You are the good in my life, and I can't lose you."

He pulled her hand to his lips and kissed her fingers. "I love you, Addie. I love you, and I don't want to spend a day without you." His voice was low and serious as he stared into her eyes.

She cupped his bearded cheek in her delicate hand as she whispered through her constricted throat, "I love you too." She knew it in her heart. In her soul.

The only love she had ever known had been with her since birth—her family. She had never made the choice to love someone before, and it was liberating. She felt the connection to him in more ways than one because he had given her more than just his love. He had given her the freedom to choose for herself.

"And I'm not leaving you. We can do this, Declan. I just have to know that you won't push me away when the darkness messes with your head. It's you and me against the world, and when you feel cheated or hurt, remember that you're not alone. You always have me."

He slowly moved toward her without breaking eye contact and kissed her furiously. He kissed her like it could be the last time, as if his life depended on it. She let him see the sincerity in her words through their kiss, their touch.

When they broke the kiss, he pulled her close and whispered, "I thought I had lost you. Losing you felt like losing myself."

"I wish your dad didn't affect you like this. He missed out. He lost. Now I've found you, and I know it would be stupid to leave you. I love you too, Declan, and we can be stronger together than we ever were apart."

"I promise I won't let him or anything else come between us. You're more important than anything else in this world, and I will always fight for you. I had a moment of weakness, and I hated it."

She knew they would still argue and disagree, but his words rang true. They knew the value in their relationship now, and it was too precious to squander.

CHAPTER TWENTY-TWO

Adeline

Declan had asked her to come home with him. The evening passed with great periods of silence between them, but she wasn't concerned. They had never felt a need to fill the void before, and now she felt that they understood each other a little better, after all was said and done. Sometimes, the hard times reveal things we need to understand about ourselves in order to begin changing for the better.

They relaxed and watched movies for hours, and she was content to just spend the time with him. Her hands traced his name over his chest in the flickering light of the television as they lay side by side on the couch. It was full dark when he finally broke the silence, and neither of them had taken the initiative to turn the light on in the living room.

He took a deep breath and confessed, "I think I could hide away with you forever."

"Of course, you would if it saved you from the torture of speaking to people in public." She laughed and kissed his chest. "I would stay here with you forever too." Her response was a whisper meant for his ears only, just as his had been only for her.

They heard Reaper barking outside, and he tensed against her. "I should let him in for the night." She knew he was thinking the same thing she was in that moment. Reaper never barked unless he felt threatened or he was unsure of a stranger. He rose to let Reaper in when his phone rang where he had left it in the kitchen.

She shivered at the cold she felt at his absence, but the feeling was heightened by Reaper's unsettling howl. They had spent the evening wrapped in soft blankets and cradled in the warmth of the couch, but it didn't feel comforting now.

She heard him answer the phone in the kitchen, his deep voice reverberating down the hall. "Hey, Five-oh."

Then there was silence. Too much silence.

She sat up on alert. Everything inside of her was screaming that something was wrong.

"We're on our way. Text me the room number," he clipped into the phone as he stomped back into the room.

"Someone broke into Karen and Butch's house tonight. They're at the hospital."

She jumped from the couch and grabbed her purse, not allowing herself to think past the necessary motions. Reaper howled again and she opened the French doors leading to the back yard to let him in before they left.

As Reaper curled around her legs to enter the house, she stopped a moment to look outside. She would have known without Reaper's harrowing howl that something was wrong. The wind was blowing, but it wasn't a full gust. She didn't hear any bugs or birds like she should. The forest was eerily quiet, and she felt watched. The claws of a predator might as well have touched the skin at the nape of her neck for all the certainty she felt. She closed the door and backed away as her instinct told her to keep alert.

She met him on the front porch and they sprinted for the truck together. He started the truck and turned to back out of the drive. She could see that Declan was all business, and he cared about her family. He would know what this would do to her if her aunt and uncle were hurt. He knew it would break her heart for the trouble she had brought to their door.

Jason would know too, and that's exactly why he would do something so horrible.

She said the words before she stopped to think what they actually meant. "He's out there."

Declan didn't look at her as he said, "I know."

She knew Reaper had sensed someone in the woods that lined Declan's property because she had sensed it herself. Jason or someone working with him was watching them, and she knew this was a trap. The alarms were shrieking in her head.

"It doesn't matter. He won't ever get to you." He said it like a fact. "Do you hear me?" He gave her a brief look that demanded an answer. The question hadn't been rhetorical. He wanted her to acknowledge his promise to her.

"I know. We're in this together." Having him by her side felt like an army standing with her. He was her first line of defense, and she rallied all of her resolve to fight beside him. If he was prepared to defend her, she would pull her own weight. He reached over and grabbed her hand in a show of solidarity.

They arrived at the hospital ten minutes later and found Karen and Butch sharing a semi-private room in the Emergency Department. Jake was standing guard outside their room, and Declan stopped to get the details from him.

She didn't know what to expect when she entered the room, but she had prepared herself for the worst. Butch and Karen were surprisingly alert. Karen was coughing through a laugh she was sharing with Butch and the deputy sitting in a chair beside her bed.

"Joe, don't make me laugh! It's painful." Karen composed herself with a few reserved coughs and noticed Addie.

"Addie, you didn't need to come up here. It's not as bad as it sounds, really... Other than the fact that they still haven't caught those heathens." Karen's tone turned sour at the end as she spat the last word.

She gently hugged her aunt and uncle. "Do they know anything?" She didn't know if she should address her aunt and uncle or the deputy.

Joe answered, "I'm afraid we don't know much, ma'am. Butch wasn't able to call us until they were long gone."

"Are the two of you all right?" she asked warily.

Karen said, "I'm fine, but the x-rays showed a fractured rib. Nothing serious, but I hope I don't have to sneeze or cough for a while." She noticed the bruises and cuts on both of their faces, but Karen must have assumed those were insignificant.

"Butch has a small fracture on his cheekbone, but there isn't anything the doctors can do for it. They said it would heal on its own, but he'll sport a nasty bruise for a while."

"Why? Why you?" Addie asked. She knew Jason had been watching her tonight at Declan's house. Why hadn't he come for her instead?

Butch answered, "One of the men started to get really rough with us, and the other man said to ease up since this was just a warning."

Karen grabbed Addie's hand. "I'm sorry, sweetie. Jake and the sheriff's department are doing everything they can to catch them."

"Did you see what they looked like?" she asked.

"No. They covered their faces. It all happened so fast. They didn't do nearly as much damage as they could have." Karen had meant to assure her, but the thought made her throat constrict.

"I'm sorry," Addie choked out.

"This is still not your fault, so don't start that." It was Butch's turn to give her the speech, but the difference this time was that she believed them.

"I know it isn't my fault. It's Jason's fault, and I'm going to put an end to this. I'm going to protect my family." She stroked Karen's hair as she promised to close the chapter in her life that had been controlled by fear.

Declan

Half an hour later, Declan had been briefed by Jake and joined them in the small exam room. Joe left them to some family time when Karen finally ran him off. He and Addie kept Butch and Karen entertained, until they were discharged a few hours later with pain medications and instructions to follow up with their primary care physician within the week.

Declan and Addie followed Butch and Karen home and helped get the two settled in bed for the night. It was well after midnight, and Declan reluctantly said his good-byes before confirming that Jake could get a deputy to ride by the house throughout the night.

Jake agreed to meet Declan at his house to help make sure Jason hadn't taken liberties while they had been gone. He knew in his bones that Jason was up to something. This break-in had been more than a warning. He just wished he knew the purpose.

He got home and found Reaper standing guard at the door instead of lounging in his bed. That was his first indication that Jason had been snooping. Reaper sniffed at him and Jake before barking and leaping, and Declan wished for once that dogs could talk.

They searched the whole house but found no signs of entry or tampering. Jake met him in the kitchen and stood with his hands on his hips. "I don't like this one bit, Dec. I know he was here, but he didn't leave a single piece of evidence. I even checked the doorknob for prints."

Maybe Jason hadn't gotten inside. Reaper would have proved to be a huge hurdle to cross. He could have just looked around the outside and schemed ways he would eventually break in. Declan rubbed his beard as he thought. "I don't know. Reaper could have scared him off."

Jake frowned. "You need an alarm system. One that doesn't just yell at you, but you need the police on call. You're a bit outside of town, and it'll take any department a few minutes to get here if you need help."

"I know. I know." He'd thought of installing a security system multiple times since Addie had come into his life. He really wished Butch and Karen had one. "I'll look into it tomorrow."

The late night was taking its toll on him, but Jake seemed on top of his game. It never ceased to amaze him how well his friend was equipped for the line of work he had chosen. Jake worked long hours and stayed alert at all times.

"Get some sleep, and don't worry about Addie tonight. I've got double duty on her house. She's being watched." Jake gave the room another once-over before shaking Declan's hand.

"Thanks, man. I really appreciate all your help."

"It's my job. I'm happy to do it. I'll be jumping for joy once we lock this guy down. I need some sleep."

After Jake left, he texted Addie. She was probably asleep by now, but his worry urged him on.

You okay?

Her response was quick.

I am. It's quiet here. Get some rest.

He wouldn't be resting tonight. He wouldn't be able to let his guard down, until Jason wasn't a threat.

Another text came through just as quickly.

I love you. Goodnight.

Something inside of him shattered. He cared for her so much. He put her safety above his own, and everything inside him was gnawing to lay eyes on her and know she was safe.

I love you too. Goodnight sweetheart.

Those words fell flat compared to the sentiment he wanted her to understand he felt. He didn't know how to fill the void in him when she was away. He wanted nothing more than to draw her in close and pass his days with her beside him.

But that's what Jason had done, wasn't it? He had chained her to him and restricted her freedom for his own selfishness. As much as he wanted more of her, he knew he couldn't take it.

Chapter Twenty-Three

Adeline

Karen came down with the flu within two days of her visit to the hospital, and Declan followed with his own immobilizing case the day after. While her aunt and her boyfriend were fading in and out of fever dreams, Addie was trying to nurse them back to health and juggle midterms.

Brian was attached to her hip per Declan's request while he was incapacitated, but she nor Brian were the least bit troubled by their forced bonding. They got along well and had an easy friendship. In fact, by the second night, Brian was calling her to plan their next day's events.

While Karen had Butch to take care of her, she still checked in on her aunt as much as possible. Addie made soup and hot tea every time she found her aunt awake and forced water at every opportunity.

As much as her aunt needed her, Declan needed her more. She had taken up the responsibility of caring for Reaper and helping out around the house. Declan hated that she was spending so much time catering to him, but she quickly hushed him up. She wanted to be here for him if he needed her, and she wasn't going anywhere.

She did come to accept that he didn't like being fussed over, so she made sure not to hover. She busied herself with laundry, cooking, cleaning, and playing with Reaper.

Brian had come by a few times to continue her self-defense lessons. It was nice having another teacher to hone the information she had been given. She was beginning to anticipate the fake attacks Declan used for practice. Although she knew Declan held back at almost every turn, Brian did her no such favors and his new perspective kept her on her toes.

Jason's warning hadn't lost its intensity, even in the hustle of the last week. Sure, she was busy, but she kept a wary eye out everywhere she went. Her instincts were on high alert, and she was having trouble sleeping. She couldn't shut her mind off to the looming threat.

She poked her head into Declan's dark room to find him stone still. She crept beside his bed to check his breathing and touched the back of her hand to his cheek and forehead to check for fever without waking him. Before leaving the room, she picked up a discarded T-shirt and decided she should probably wash a load of clothes for him.

Keeping busy had been the only way to keep herself calm in the wake of the break-in at Karen and Butch's house. Addie leaned over to shove the clothing into the washing machine, but she jerked upright and turned on a dime when she thought she heard a noise behind her. In the second after her adrenaline-filled jump, she found no one in sight. Not even Reaper. She immediately wondered if she had heard anything at all or if the stress of waiting for Jason to seek her out again was getting the best of her.

She couldn't shake the feeling someone was watching her. Even when she stepped into the small hallway of Declan's house where no one could possibly hide, she felt tracked. The weight of an invisible stare settled in her gut.

She was being hunted.

She poked her head into Declan's room again and found him in the same position she had left him. Likewise, Reaper was nestled in his bed in the living room. Breathing easier, she chided herself for her worry. If Reaper wasn't worried, she shouldn't be either. He had better senses than she did.

"You wanna play some fetch in the backyard?" Reaper's ears perked up, and he led her to the French doors in the kitchen.

When she opened the doors, her attention was drawn to the dense tree line to her right. It was the beginning of September, but the weather hadn't yet turned in northern Georgia, and the trees were still full and green. The opaque green canopy turned the forest floor into a mysterious void.

She knew Reaper didn't like being locked up in the house day and night, but what risk could she be taking by standing around outdoors when Jason was known to take advantage of opportunities like this one.

Her gaze followed the intricate branches of the oaks and pines to the sky where the crows wove a winding dance back and forth over the forest. Her first thought was that she didn't need an omen as obvious as a murder of crows to know her time was short. She shook the superstition from her mind and reminded herself it wasn't uncommon to see crows dotting the skies of any southern state.

But the birds of the night weren't the only strangeness in the woods. Stepping off the porch to follow Reaper into the yard, she scanned the trees with an intensity she felt was necessary given her current situation. She was drawn to the immense forest and couldn't look away. It was too large, too cavernous, and too…

It was quiet. Reaper's bark could be heard echoing faintly off the hills, but no sound came from the woods. Addie fully believed that God had given every creature at least some form of self-preservation, and she could feel it now as she scanned the silent forest before her.

Should she remind herself that she herself was a creature of God's own making, and one that had been given instincts to survive and thrive?

When she was sure she could hear her own heartbeat, she realized that even Reaper's barking had ceased. She turned to find the German Shepherd standing five feet to her left and trained on the woods just as she had been moments before.

That was enough confirmation for her. "Come on, Reaper. Let's get back inside." She turned to ascend the stairs, but the dog didn't follow. "Reaper. Come." He reluctantly turned from the quiet forest and dashed inside before she had fully opened the door.

There was a hunter in those woods, and she had never felt more vulnerable.

Declan recovered before the end of the week and didn't waste time jumping back into work. The salon had officially closed for reconstruction two days ago, and Addie was already getting nervous about her financial situation. She and Karen had gone over her budget more than once, but the all-too-familiar feeling of helplessness crept in when she remembered her lack of income.

Karen and Butch had been more than willing to pay for her classes and had assured her they didn't expect repayment. She had openly wept when they first broke the news to her, but they explained to her that it would be an honor to pitch in some of their savings for her education. She was the closest they had to a child themselves, and Butch liked to remind her that were his sister still alive, she would disown him if he let her daughter go without.

Still, as generous and selfless as the gift was, Addie felt like she wasn't moving forward if she wasn't helping herself. Her lack of education was her own fault. Her parents had set her up for college and a solid life, and she had mistrusted someone in her time of grief. Sure, she could blame Jason for taking what was rightfully hers, but she had practically given all that money away when she made a terrible decision in her naivety.

With the salon closed for at least a month and only studying left to do, guitar lessons with Brian had become something to look forward to. The lessons were a community affair. She and Brian met at Rusty's before opening hours to practice, and Declan and their friends tended to file in as soon as they were off the clock in the afternoons.

The week after Declan was recovered from the flu, she walked into Rusty's for her lesson. The chairs were stacked on the tabletops as usual, but one table was occupied by Brian and Paul, the owner of Rusty's. To her surprise, Declan stood behind Brian with his thick arms crossed over his chest.

She couldn't tell from her first assessment if the gathering of the three was for good or bad purposes, but once Declan noticed her entrance, all of her worries faded away. His eyes were bright, and his smile was genuine. She was relieved to see his strength back after the sickness he had suffered, and she appreciated every healthy minute she shared with him.

"Hey, guys."

Paul stood at her approach but didn't give away the meaning of his presence. She had met the robust man a couple of times before, but she hadn't shared more than pleasantries with him. It wasn't a secret around town that the restaurant owner was a long-time member of the local motorcycle club, and Rusty's was one of a handful of businesses managed by the MC. The club didn't cause problems around town, and they organized quite a few charity events in the area. Still, she felt completely at ease around Paul with his burned-charcoal beard and protruding beer belly.

"Nice to see you again, Adeline. You stayin' out of trouble?"

Something in Paul's demeanor reminded her of her father. It was probably the way he always asked how she was doing and seemed to truly care about her answer, or maybe it was the smell of barbecue and tobacco that brought back memories. "I'm doing well, Paul. How's the business?"

"Business is business as usual. Not much changes 'round here."

Brian rubbed his hands together and tried to contain a megawatt smile. "Just get to the point and tell her already."

"Tell me what?" she asked.

Paul's attention seemed to be anywhere except on Addie as he rubbed the back of his neck and stumbled over his words. "Well, you see, Brian has been talking you up for a bit now, and he thinks we should bring you in for a set tomorrow night."

Her squeal filled the empty bar before the last word was out of the owner's mouth. "Really? I'm in?"

Brian stood to hug her. "You're in, Addie. We've been working on a dozen duets for a couple of weeks now, and I like our sound. I told Declan I thought it would be a good idea to bring you on stage, and he wanted to be here to see your reaction."

She turned to Declan, who had been watching patiently a few feet away. "I can't believe this is happening!" She ran to him, and he caught her in midair. While clinging to the man she loved in what could be the happiest moment of her life, she silently thanked God for dragging her from the darkness into the light.

Declan released her, but his smile lingered. "I'm not surprised. I've heard you sing many times now, and you have a gift. I think it's a great idea to share it with everyone."

Brian slapped her hard on the shoulder. "Yeah, but I don't think you're ready to play yet. Let's stick to singing for now."

She laughed. "You're right. I'm not ready. A few weeks isn't enough to make me comfortable playing in front of dozens of people. Thank you, Brian." She turned to Paul. "Thank you both. I'm so honored."

Both men nodded, and Brian pulled a folded piece of paper from his back pocket. "I was thinking these would be some good songs to start on. We can practice today and tomorrow after your class, and I think you'll be more than ready to take the stage."

At the mention of the stage, Addie turned to take in the raised area in the corner of the dining hall. The crude platform stood only two feet taller than the rest of the floor, but the elevation made all the difference. She knew the way that stage lit up on weekend nights. She knew the music would envelop her into a cocoon of bliss. She knew the thump of Brian's boots on the knotted floorboards. The vibrations were as real to her now as they were during a performance.

Soon, she would be a part of the show. She would be sharing her talent, and the giddiness bubbled inside her. She cupped her hands over her mouth and whispered almost to herself again, "I can't believe this is happening."

Declan stood behind her, but her feet were rooted to the wooden floorboards by her shock. His hands gripped her shoulders and gently pulled her to rest against his chest. "You're going to be great up there. I'm so proud of you."

She knew in her bones that he truly was proud of her, and she knew her mom and dad would feel the same sense of pride had they been here to share this moment with her. Her parents had known how much singing meant to her, just as Declan knew her dreams. How rare was it to find someone in life that wanted the best for you at every turn? How lucky must she be to have stumbled upon someone as selfless as Declan King?

It wasn't luck at all. It was fate. A fortuitous blessing that had brought them together.

She turned to him and hugged him tight. "Thank you."

"I didn't do this. You did."

She was finally beginning to feel like she truly was making her own way. Her hard work with Brian these last few weeks was paying off, and she was beginning to see the happiness ahead.

CHAPTER TWENTY-FOUR

Declan

Addie and Brian were supposed to perform, starting at eight that evening. Declan was still playing catch-up at work, but he rushed home for a shower before heading to Rusty's. He hated that he couldn't be with her while she waited impatiently for her first on-stage show, but she had assured him she was doing fine.

He had called her to check in when he was leaving work, and he could tell she was nervous. She was distracted, and he could hear the strain in her voice. He called Brian as he locked up the house to head over to the bar.

Declan asked, "Hey, how's the star?"

The music from the jukebox was drowning out every other word Brian spoke. "She's hanging on, but I'm going to start worrying if she doesn't start speaking in complete sentences soon. All I've heard from her for the last hour is 'uh huh' and 'nuh-uh.'"

Declan stopped with his hand on the door handle of the truck. "Does she need me to bring her anything?"

"Nah. Just some oxygen. She looks like she might hyperventilate."

"Just tell her I'm on my way. Call me back if she needs anything."

"See you in a sec."

He disconnected the call and grabbed his baseball cap from the console of the truck. He should have been there for her today. He knew better than anyone how difficult it could be to stand in front of an audience. After all, it usually only took one person to make him sweaty and splotchy.

He shoved the cap onto his head and thought about how much easier his life had become since he met Addie. Sure, he lived in a constant state of worry about her and the crazy ex-boyfriend who followed her around, but she had changed him in ways he never knew possible.

He could actually go out in public without hesitating or second guessing himself.

He had jumped into his truck tonight headed for a crowded restaurant without thinking twice. Not only that, but he couldn't wait to get there because she would be waiting for him. Sometimes, the risk was well worth the reward.

When he stepped through the door at Rusty's, his gaze scanned the overcrowded bar for Addie's chestnut waves. He didn't have to look far. He could always pick her out of a crowd. She wore a white, crochet sundress and brown cowboy boots tonight, and he was once again irritated at himself for being delayed.

He made a path through the bar patrons toward her, but she spotted him before he made it to the table where she was sitting. Their friends were huddled around her laughing and joking in the jovial night air.

She stood from her chair without a word and met him halfway. "I'm glad you're here."

If she only knew how glad he was to be here himself. "I wouldn't miss it. Are you all set?"

"Yeah, Brian and I set up earlier. It really doesn't take long." He could hear the uneven cadence of her voice and worried she would be too nervous to enjoy the fun in this night.

"Come here. I missed you today." He pulled her into a hug and thought about what it meant to miss Addie while he was at work for a few hours. He had missed his family and friends in the years he had been away from home, but missing Addie when they were apart felt much the same, despite the discrepancy between the lengths of time.

He missed his mother, the same way he always would, but that loss couldn't be remedied with a quick visit.

The clock above the bar read a quarter till eight. Addie would take the stage soon, and he wanted to soak up as much of her for himself as he could. They didn't move, didn't rejoin their friends at the table. He held her until he could feel her muscles loosening beneath his arms and her breathing flowing in and out in steady streams.

When she raised her head to look up at him, he could see the wonder in her eyes. He had something to tell her, and it couldn't wait any longer. "Guess what?"

She smiled. "Don't make me guess."

"I took your advice. I called my dad today."

Her eyes opened wide and she stepped back to look at him. "Really? What did he say?"

Declan shrugged. "Not much. I just told him I was sorry for cutting him off when he came by."

She prodded, "And?"

"And he said he was sorry for leaving Mom and me and he wanted to get to know me again. I told him I don't know if I'm ready just yet, but we can keep in touch a bit and see how things go."

Her mouth hung open in a stunned smile. "I'm so happy for you, Declan."

"It's a start. All because of you." He kissed her on the top of her head just as Brian stood up from his seat at the table. "You ready, Addie?"

"I think I'm ready."

Declan kissed her ruby lips and squeezed her hip before whispering, "I know you're ready."

She backed away from him until her fingers slipped from his hand. He followed her to the table where Brian stood waiting for her. His friend gestured to the stage with a nod, and she followed him to the platform.

The noise of the crowd was choked out as Brian sat on the barstool in front of a microphone and Addie adjusted her own to the same position it had been in when she first began touching it. He could see her blush clearly beneath the spotlight as her lithe fingers caressed the microphone stand.

"Good evening, everyone." Shouts and cheers rang from the crowd at Brian's greeting. "Y'all ready to hear some tunes tonight?" Another wave of screams filled the air.

"I've got a partner with me tonight. Let's give Adeline Rhodes a warm welcome." The cheers for Addie rivaled the last two rounds, and he could see her grin split her face.

"We've been practicing together for a little while now, and you're gonna love the flavor she brings to the weekly pot around here. I think you'll enjoy this first number, and it's fitting for Addie's first song."

The claps and whistles quieted as Brian began to play a distinctly country song on his guitar. As Addie's voice joined the tune, Declan recognized the song as one his mother used to love playing in the car when he was young. He agreed that Reba McEntire's "Is There Life Out There" was a fitting song for Addie to sing tonight.

She and Brian nailed every song. She sang some solo, and others Brian joined her in a duet. Declan hung around his friends while Addie was on stage, but there were a few times in the night when he found himself telling the bartender or a

JUST AS I AM | **311**

waitress that the beautiful brunette on stage was his girlfriend.

When Brian and Addie descended the stage, hordes of people flocked to congratulate them and fawn over Brian's new partner. Declan could tell this wouldn't be the last time Addie would be performing, if the fanfare had anything to say about it.

When she reached their table, her entire face was red, and her eyes were sparkling. "That was amazing!"

His excitement matched hers as he added, "I know. Everyone loved it. You really have a talent, Addie."

She expelled a deep breath and reached for her glass of lukewarm water where she left it on the table and swallowed three gulps. The excitement was dying from the performance, but the noise hadn't dimmed when she grabbed his arm to get his attention.

"I'm exhausted. You want to go home?"

He was sure the tension of waiting to play tonight coupled with the strain of singing for hours would be enough to leave most people tired. "Sure. I'm ready when you are."

"I rode with Brian, but I left my car at your house."

"I know. I ran by the house after work to get cleaned up."

Brian popped up beside him with a slap on the shoulder. "You did great, Addie. We're definitely doing that again." Brian turned his attention back to Declan. "Hey, I'm gonna give Marcus a ride to your place to pick up pop's truck. He said he'd have some time to work on it tomorrow and doesn't want to have to worry about getting a ride."

"Sure, man. Addie and I were just about to head that way."

Brian pointed to Marcus seated a few tables over. "We'll just follow you. Marcus has to get home 'cause his brother Brandon has football practice in the morning."

"No problem."

They walked outside into a torrential summer rain. The exterior lights in the parking lot cast a hazy glow in the downpour, and they ran to Declan's truck just as Brian and Marcus made a dash for Brian's Jeep.

They were panting and dripping wet before they reached the truck and shoved themselves inside. The doors slammed shut in unison and they turned to each other in the cloak of silence and laughed. When the interior light dimmed to darkness in the cab of the truck, they still didn't move.

She breathed, "This was the best night of my life."

He gripped the back of her neck beneath her wet hair and whispered, "Mine too."

It really had been a night to remember. Having Addie by his side made every moment better than the last, and he was learning that life was more than just getting by.

Chapter Twenty-Five

Adeline

They pulled into the drive, and Reaper's frantic barking could be heard from inside the house over the torrential rain. Declan tensed beside her, but she knew something was wrong too. For the first time, she had forgotten about Jason and the threat he posed. She sang for a crowd, laughed with her friends, and had fallen deeper in love with Declan tonight. Would Jason really take her from the happiest night of her life and remind her that the devil she was running from never rests?

Declan shifted the truck to park and squeezed her hand. "Wait for me to come around and get you, then stay beside me." He was in no hurry as he stepped out of the truck into the rain and met with Marcus before coming to get her. She stepped into the torrent, and her clothes were instantly drenched. She couldn't see anything through the dark and the rain.

She watched Marcus and Brian bound up the porch stairs for the front entrance, while Declan led her to the backdoor. They expected trouble, and she knew he would search the whole house before settling in with her.

He wasn't going to let her out of his sight, and he kept a tight grip on her hand as they waded through the mud. She knew that he was armed, but she felt completely defenseless herself. The bare bones of her training with him felt like child's play, and the knife clipped inside her boot felt too heavy. Could she bring herself to use it if Jason was really coming for her?

Declan opened the back door but didn't let go of her hand. He looked back into the rainy night of the backyard before turning his attention to the house again. She couldn't tell if it was quiet inside or not. The rain was deafening against the tin roof.

Declan opened the French door and tugged her close behind him as he entered the house. Before she could step in, cold hands grabbed her from behind, pulling her over the railing of the deck before she could regain her grip on Declan's hand. She screamed just as he turned to grab for her, but two more men emerged from the shadows beneath the deck and pulled him back as he lunged for her outstretched arms.

She was propelled backward over the rail before landing hard enough on her back to push all of the air from her lungs. She gasped for breath as rain flowed over her face, knowing she had to prepare herself for whatever Jason had planned for her. She hoped death was quick and painless, but she couldn't bring herself to pray for a swift end as Jason's shadow loomed over her. Still, she hoped the part of her that registered pain died first.

She panted to refill her lungs with air and risked taking her attention from Jason to search for Declan. She could see him on the deck holding his own against two men, but she knew he would only be able to keep them at bay for so long if they had weapons.

More movement drew her attention as Brian threw the back door open and released Reaper who attacked the men attempting to restrain Declan. Once Declan broke the hold of one man completely, he used the free hand to land a knockout punch to the other's face. The man fell like a stone statue, and she felt a slight relief knowing that he would have no trouble handling the other attacker alone.

A battle seemed to be raging behind him, but Jason was fixated on her. He moved slowly toward her, blocking her from seeing the people she had come to care for more deeply than she knew possible. She crawled away without turning her back to him, but she was only buying herself precious seconds of safety.

A deafening shot broke the night, and what little air she had gained back died in her throat. Her heart stopped for an extended moment as Brian was thrown off his feet by the force of the bullet.

Jason stood with the same eerie stillness above her and lowered the gun to his side.

Her scream pierced the air as blood rushed in her head. She heard the scream as if she were underwater. "No!"

Jason spat in her face, but the rage in his voice was tempered by the torrential downpour. "Shut up!" Her arm was jerked behind her, and the butt of the gun crushed into her face.

Specks of light danced like illuminated flying insects in the night as Jason stood over her holding the warm barrel to her temple.

Brian... She couldn't finish the thought. To give life to the horrible thought would make it true.

Jason pushed her, but she caught herself with her hands as her body rushed toward the soggy ground. The whimper that escaped from her mouth was weak as she made contact with the earth, and her anger boiled. She had sworn he would never touch her again, and the hit had been more than a slap in the face. It had meant a small victory for him, and she decided she couldn't allow it to end that way. She would be the final victor—for herself, for her freedom, and for her friend who had been shot tonight because he willingly put himself in danger to protect her.

She felt at her boot for the knife Declan had given her and discreetly gripped it with a prayer for accuracy. She heard Jason approaching behind her as his soggy footsteps sent chills up her wet spine.

She was at war with herself just as she battled against Jason. Her body rebelled against the thought of hurting someone, even the one who had caused her so much grief. Despite the wrongs he had done to her, regardless of the pain he had caused her, her stomach turned at the realization of what she would have to do to protect herself.

When she could feel him closing in behind her, she turned to stab the blade into his thigh. It sank deep and her mind warred with the instinct to retreat from the violence and the deep-seeded anger she felt toward him.

Jason wailed in pain as she made up her mind and quickly twisted the blade only a fraction of an inch before jerking it free. A river of blood slithered down his jeans and quickly spread outward. She pulled her arm back to see if she would have to stab him again when a bulking form sailed above where she crouched on the ground and collided with Jason. It had all happened too fast to process, but her mind and body were still on high alert.

Her wet hair stuck to her face as she scrambled to her feet to see Declan pinning Jason to the muddy earth. The light from the house cast an eerie glow on the dominant fighter towering above his conquered foe.

CHAPTER TWENTY - SIX

Declan

Unfamiliar rage had boiled inside him as he bolted from the deck toward Addie and Jason in the backyard.

How dare he touch her. How dare he come for her here where she should be safe. Declan had known he loved her that night he held her under the stars, and he wouldn't allow her to be lost in the same place he had found himself.

He had always been able to control his emotions, but he had never seen a man hit a woman until Addie came into his life. Now, he knew that his control meant nothing when someone threatened the woman he loved. He had known since the moment he met her that he would do anything to protect her. He would fight for her, die for her… kill for her.

When he tackled Jason to the ground, he pinned the man beneath him and let his anger ride the punches. Jason made a pitiful attempt to protect himself, but Declan had trained to box since he was in high school.

"No! Declan, wait!" Her scream was urgent enough to cut through the dying rain.

Addie shakily found her footing in the wet grass and ran to him, and he struggled to pull his next punch, then stopped the next midair and lowered his fist.

She was shaking violently when he turned to her, and something in him broke apart knowing he hadn't shielded her from enough. Least of all himself.

"I don't want you to… I don't want you to hurt him. I just want him to…" She turned her attention to Jason, who gasped for breath through gritted teeth. He was covered in mud and blood that even the rain couldn't wash away.

"I just want you to leave me alone." Even the weather couldn't hide her tears. He could hear her hurt in every word she spoke. "Please, just leave me alone. That's all I want."

The warning of sirens pierced the night, and the flashing blue and red lights followed.

Jason screamed, "No!" but Jake, Joe, and two other deputies Declan didn't recognize rounded the corner of the house just as Addie placed a hand on his shoulder. He knew she was trying to tell him to back away from Jason, but he didn't want to break his hold on the danger that had been lurking in their life.

When Jake pulled him away from Jason, he kept his distance from Addie. The cloud of anger was receding, and he was beginning to regret the extent he had gone to in front of her.

She only hesitated a moment before stepping to him and touching his arm. When he followed her line of sight, he saw a thick gash bisecting his arm. In the heat of battle, he hadn't even noticed.

"Are you all right? Declan, I was so afraid. I lost sight of you, and I…"

He grabbed her into a crushing embrace and held her tight, attempting to make up for so many failures. He was still seeing red and probably shaking himself with the need to release his fury, so he kissed the top of her wet head and prayed for peace from the storm boiling inside him.

"He was going to kill me." She said the words without emotion. They were a matter of fact, and the truth of how differently this night could have ended hit him in the gut. He couldn't stop her body from shaking, no matter how tightly he held her.

"I don't know if I could have stopped him," she whispered so low he barely heard her over the dying rain.

"I wouldn't have let that happen, but it looked like you had the situation handled." He stroked her hair and took a deep breath. "I can't live without you, Addie." He was almost crushing her now, but he didn't care. He never wanted to let her go again. He could have lost the only woman he had ever loved tonight.

Sobs began to shudder through her body, and he continued to hold her. He rubbed her back as she cried loudly and passionately for the narrow escape they had made.

Finally, a mumbled word escaped with the sobs. "Brian…"

"I'm not sure how Brian is doing, but Marcus is with him. Let's just deal with this one thing at a time, sweetheart. It's over, and now we have to find a way to go forward from here." He really didn't know if Brian had survived that shot, but he had to keep hope alive until they knew otherwise. He wasn't ready to face that loss.

He looked at the sky as he held her in the misting rain. The stars were hidden by clouds, and a part of him was glad. Something was shielding the beauty from this bloody mess tonight, and it seemed right that way.

"What about…" She tried to look behind her, but he grabbed her shoulders to stop her.

"He's in Jake's hands now." He didn't know what the future held for Jason, but he was glad that judgment and punishment weren't his duties. He knew the decision he had almost made in the heat of the moment. In the second he had made that decision, he had known he couldn't get to Addie quickly enough, and he wouldn't risk giving Jason an opportunity to touch her again. He couldn't conceive of giving Jason an inch when it came to Addie. *His* Addie. The one who had saved him.

"Let's get you inside so you can dry off." Maybe if she could get comfortable, she would feel marginally better after what happened here tonight.

The first time he told her he loved her, he had meant it with his whole heart, and he loved her more now, if that was even possible. Was this the course of their relationship? If so, he didn't know how long he could continue to love her exponentially. At some point, it might just consume him.

She let him lead her inside where they found a paramedic readying supplies to administer treatment. Brian was laid across a gurney, bloody and unconscious. Declan didn't restrain his sigh of relief when Marcus nodded that Brian would be all right. Marcus stood to meet them, and Declan quickly assessed him for injuries before shaking his hand.

"The EMT said it doesn't look too bad from his first evaluation. He was hit in the shoulder, so no major organs were compromised. He may not even need surgery. We'll know more when he gets to the hospital," Marcus filled them in quickly.

"Thanks, brother." The words would never convey the meaning they should hold. His friends had always had his back, but he had never asked them to risk their lives before. He felt incredibly lucky to have so many loyal friends at his side.

CHAPTER TWENTY-SEVEN

Adeline

She waited out of the way while the EMT wheeled Brian to the ambulance. She would be forever grateful for the risks her friends had taken tonight, and she made a vow that Brian would always have her support. He had released Reaper, allowing Declan to gain the advantage he needed, and he had taken a bullet at great risk for her.

How many people would be as selfless as Brian had been tonight?

How many people would make the decision to place himself between her and danger like Declan had done?

She was alive tonight because she had stumbled into a circle of people of the most selfless kind. Only her family had ever loved her as fiercely and truly as Declan, and she had never dreamed of experiencing a friendship as meaningful and deep as the ones she was a part of now.

For the first time, she wondered what would become of Jason. It suddenly felt like a weight around her neck that she hadn't tried harder to help him. She should have prayed for him. Prayed for him sooner than this moment. She had been so wrapped up in her own problems and hadn't spared a thought for him. Her heart pounded as she feared it was too late. She decided to ask Jake if it would be possible to pass a Bible or at least some scripture or encouraging devotionals to him wherever he ended up.

Marcus had stayed by her side as police and paramedics buzzed around them doing their jobs. He had been as comforting as he was capable of being, but it just wasn't in his makeup to be the soothing type. She understood completely. She was simply glad he was by her side. They each gave formal statements to one of the deputies before Jake entered the house after checking for any more of Jason's friends.

She had been numb in the wake of the life-altering events of the night, but as Declan stood beside her like a powerful guardian, his presence was beginning to bring her back to life. Their eyes met, and his gaze told her so much. He wouldn't forget this easily. It would be an event they would have to work past together, and she had no doubt they would face it head-on.

He gathered her into a soul-crushing hug again, as if he still needed to touch her to reassure himself she was real and whole. "I'm all right," she whispered to alleviate some of his anxiety.

"I'm going to make sure you stay that way."

They made their way to the hospital to check on Brian, as soon as they had showered and washed the filth and blood of the night from their bodies. Neither of them had slept, but she was grateful for the short nap she had taken the evening before.

They reached Brian's room just as a pretty young nurse stepped out and greeted them. "He's just out of recovery, and the anesthesia has him a little sluggish. He's really doing great, considering the injury he sustained."

Addie's shoulders fell in relief. "Thank you for letting us know, and thank you for taking care of him."

The nurse laughed. "That one is a riot. He's been a pleasure to attend."

When they stepped into the room, Brian didn't even try to hide the lazy grin on his pale face. His smile didn't hold his usual sparkle of humor, but it calmed her to know some things never change.

Brian reached for her hand as she stepped into the room. "She's got the hots for me."

Addie's vision went glassy in relief. "I don't see how she could possibly resist you."

Declan stepped beside her and wrapped his arm around her shoulder. "How you holdin' up, man?"

"It hurts, but I'll survive. Don't tell the nurse I said that. She thinks I'm dying." He winked at Addie, and she released a shaky giggle. If someone had told her a few hours ago she would be joking with Brian right now, she would have called them a liar. Now, she couldn't help but be immensely thankful for everything.

"Brian, thank you." She stopped as her vision clouded with unshed tears again.

"Hey, hey, hey. Listen, Addie. I would do anything for you. You don't get to come into our lives and make us better for knowing you without getting the perks. We look after our own. By the way, remind me to stay on your good side. I heard you stabbed the guy."

An uncertain laugh sprang from her throat, and she let the tears fall.

"Just try not to get me shot again." His eyes drifted closed, and she grabbed his hand, wishing she could hug him.

Declan rubbed her back gently, and she knew this was home.

They stepped out of the hospital a quarter of an hour later into the blinding morning sun. She raised her hand to shield her eyes. The sun had risen and the town was bustling with morning frenzy. "I'm starving." She was running on fumes, but the exertion of the night had left her ravenous.

"I'll take you anywhere you want to go." He wrapped his muscular arm around her shoulders to pull her closer as they walked.

She chose The Line, since she knew it was one of Declan's favorite places too. They chose a booth in the far corner of the restaurant, even though most of the tables were empty this morning. They sank into their seats like melting butter at the same time and laughed at the novelty of the moment. They were relaxing in a restaurant without the need to keep an eye out for danger, and the sweet feeling of victory danced in both of their eyes.

As they sat in companionable silence, neither of them wanted to talk about the previous night and its horrors. It was behind them, and going back would be toxic.

When they had finished their breakfast and a few cups of coffee, he leaned over the table to grab her hands. He was looking at her with mixed emotions, and she knew he wouldn't be able to think straight until the bruise on her cheek healed. It was a sneaky reminder of the pain of the past, but unlike Declan's scars, this one would fade.

He cupped her chin to grab her attention. "Addie, I know without a doubt that I don't want to live a day without you in my life. I know we were thrown together for a reason far greater than what we came through last night."

"I know," she confessed. They knew each other now better than ever. She had shared more of herself with Declan than any other person in the world, and their bond was stronger for it.

"I don't have a ring, and I don't want to pressure you into making a quick decision. We have our whole lives to get married, but I want you to know that I want that for us. One day. When you're ready." He rubbed his calloused thumb over the back of her hand. "I know what I want, and it's you. I won't ever want anyone else.

I love you with every fiber of my being, and I want you in my life forever."

He had laid himself out for her, and she loved what she saw. He was selfless, loyal, loving, and honest. He would be her other half from now on, and she couldn't be happier.

She could divide her life into two sections: her life with him and her life without him. When she had been scared and alone, and when she was loved and cherished. When she was lost, and when she was found. Before, when she had lived in fear and never thought to pray for deliverance, and after, when she knew the comfort of giving her life over to God and His plan for her.

She had made enough life-changing decisions in the last few months to last her a while, but she was happy to make one more to secure the happiness she had fought so hard to know. This was her cornerstone. The moment her future would build on. The choice that would be the foundation for the life she planned to build with Declan.

And she was more than happy to take this chance. She would gladly take a chance on life and love and happiness. There wasn't another option for her. Every obstacle she had come through had been worth it all to have the happiness that stood before her now.

Her bruised face pulled tight with her smile, but she would give herself to him as he had given himself to her. "I don't know how I could have been missing someone I had never known, but a part of me craved you in my life long before I met you. New Orleans was the only home I had ever known." She squeezed his hand to make sure he heard her. "You are my home now."

He pulled her hand until they were both standing and pulled her in close. "Let's go home."

ABOUT THE AUTHOR

Mandi Blake was born and raised in Alabama where she lives with her husband and daughter, but her southern heart loves to travel. Reading has been her favorite hobby for as long as she can remember, but writing is her passion. She loves a good happily ever after in her sweet Christian romance books and loves to see her characters relationships grow closer to God and each other.

Thank you so much for reading *Just as I am*. I hope you loved reading it as much as I enjoyed writing it! I want to thank you for taking a chance on a new author. If you loved the book, stay tuned for more in the Unfailing Love series.

If you want to connect with me, visit my website here: www.mandiblakeauthor.com.